Hi, Aubrey. Ha—
I have good news—I finally have time for
you. I promise we'll have fun—or at least
I will. See you soon.

The words played like a drumbeat in her head. She gripped the edge of the table hard enough to make her hands ache. It was the best way to stop herself from sliding onto the floor to curl up in a ball of pure terror.

When she could draw a full breath, Aubrey carefully refolded the note and shoved both it and the box back into the padded envelope. Then, hoping to find a moment of peace, she closed her eyes and offered up a prayer asking God for strength and guidance. As always, putting her trust in Him helped her feel centered and back in control. Taking another deep breath, she put the envelope in her canvas bag, grabbed her purse and headed for the door.

It might have been smarter to call the police, but she didn't want them swarming all over her home. It was her sanctuary, and she was careful who she let come inside. No, she would go to them and share the news. Finally, after twelve years, her cold case had just turned hot.

USA TODAY bestselling author **Alexis Morgan** has always loved reading and now spends her days creating worlds filled with strong heroes and gutsy heroines. She is the author of over fifty novels, novellas and short stories that span a wide variety of genres: American West historicals; paranormal and fantasy romances; cozy mysteries; and contemporary romances. More information about her books can be found on her website, alexismorgan.com.

Books by Alexis Morgan

Love Inspired Suspense

A Lethal Truth

Love Inspired The Protectors

The Reluctant Guardian

Harlequin Heartwarming

Heroes of Dunbar Mountain

The Lawman's Promise
To Trust a Hero

Visit the Author Profile page at LoveInspired.com for more titles.

A Lethal Truth

ALEXIS MORGAN

LOVE INSPIRED SUSPENSE
INSPIRATIONAL ROMANCE

LOVE INSPIRED® SUSPENSE
INSPIRATIONAL ROMANCE

Recycling programs
for this product may
not exist in your area.

ISBN-13: 978-1-335-98024-3

A Lethal Truth

Love Inspired
22 Adelaide St. West, 41st Floor
Toronto, Ontario M5H 4E3, Canada
www.LoveInspired.com

Printed in Lithuania

MIX
Paper | Supporting
responsible forestry
FSC® C021394

Be strong and of a good courage, fear not, nor be afraid of them: for the Lord thy God, he it is that doth go with thee; he will not fail thee, nor forsake thee.
—*Deuteronomy* 31:6

To my wonderful agent Michelle Grajkowski—
thank you so much for always encouraging me to try
something new. And to my friend Janice Kay Johnson—
thanks for always being there when I need to
bring a new story to life.

ONE

As far as Aubrey Sims was concerned, it was pretty much a toss-up who was more excited about the fact that there were only two weeks left in the school year—the kids or their teachers. While she dearly loved her third grade students, keeping them focused on their classwork pretty much burned up every ounce of energy she had. Right now, all she wanted to do was go home, fix a snack and put her feet up for a while.

Unfortunately, she had a couple of errands to run before any of that could happen. So far, she'd gotten gas and picked up enough groceries to last until the weekend. That left just one more stop—her weekly visit to the post office to pick up her mail. It wasn't exactly convenient, but she preferred to have it delivered somewhere other than directly to her house. After all, a single woman could never be too careful.

Inside the post office lobby, Aubrey unlocked her box and dropped all of the mail into the canvas bag she'd brought in from the car. There was also a key for one of the larger boxes the post office used for oversize items. When she unlocked it, inside was a padded envelope addressed to her.

Aubrey studied the envelope and frowned. She gave it a

gentle squeeze and thought maybe it held a small box. She hadn't ordered anything recently, but maybe her mother had wanted to surprise her with something. On second thought, that didn't seem likely. Her birthday was still months away, and there weren't any upcoming holidays that warranted a gift. That was a puzzle to solve later. For now, Aubrey dropped the envelope into her bag, more than ready to be done for the day.

On the drive home, she found herself glancing at her canvas bag and wondering about the unexpected envelope. What on earth could it be? As much as she wanted to learn the answer to that question, other things had to take priority. Once she was parked in her driveway, she concentrated on carrying in the groceries as well as the stuff she'd brought home from school to work on that evening.

Once everything was inside, Aubrey carefully engaged the two locks on the front door, fastened the security chain, and finally turned the dead bolt. The security system showed no alerts, but still she did a quick inspection of every room. She hated being so paranoid, but when something unexpected happened—however innocent—it sometimes triggered a powerful compulsion to check inside the closets and even under the beds.

Satisfied that she was safe, Aubrey dumped all of her mail out on the dining room table to sort. Junk mail went into the recycling bin while the bills joined the stack next to her computer. That left the mystery envelope. To postpone opening it a little longer, she fixed herself a glass of ice water before sitting down at the table. There, she picked up the mysterious envelope and studied it. Her name and address was written with a felt tip pen, the handwriting sloppy and not very professional-looking. The more she studied it, the more uncomfortable she became, and her curiosity morphed into something closer to dread.

It was tempting to get up and walk away, but delaying would accomplish nothing. After taking a deep breath, she gently tugged on the tear strip that would open the envelope. It took her two tries to rip it off completely. Peeking inside, she saw that she'd been right about the small box. It was the size and style that might hold earrings or possibly a necklace. Tipping the padded envelope over, she let the box and a pink envelope slide out onto the table.

Which should she open first? Not that it really mattered. She really hated that her hand was shaking when she gently lifted off the lid off the box. Nestled in a layer of padding was a rare coin, a type Aubrey recognized on sight. She'd only seen one other like it in her lifetime, but the image had been burned into her memory forever.

Chills ran up and down her spine as she quickly shoved the lid back onto the box. The truth was that even out of sight the coin had the ability to terrify her. That was because other than the police, there was only one person who understood the significance of a buffalo nickel in Aubrey's life. And if the coin was scary, the accompanying note would likely be far worse.

The pink envelope was the size that normally held greeting cards or maybe fancy stationery. Even without opening it, she sensed her life going off the rails again, but ignoring the threat wouldn't help. Experience had taught her that the only way to deal with life-altering disasters was to keep moving forward one step at a time. She forced herself to pick up the envelope to see what she could learn from it.

The sender had tucked the flap inside the envelope rather than sealing it shut. That made sense. He—and she was sure it was a "he"—probably hadn't wanted to risk giving the authorities his DNA by licking the envelope. Her name had been written in the same messy handwriting, but this time with a ballpoint pen.

Having learned all she could from the envelope, she reluctantly moved onto the note inside. Taking great care not to damage it, she unfolded the paper and set it back down on the table. Before reading it, she stopped to sip some water, hoping to ease the huge lump in her throat. It didn't work. Rather than try again, she turned her focus to the message on the paper. At first, she couldn't make sense of what it said even though the writing was legible and the words correctly spelled.

No, the problem was that her brain wasn't functioning properly and couldn't string the individual words together into any kind of coherent message. Maybe reading them aloud would help. It took a second try before anything began to make sense. Horrible, terrible, terrifying sense. She found herself being plunged back into the middle of a nightmare that had begun twelve years before and changed her life forever.

There were differences this time. Back then the words had been spoken to her face, not written in an anonymous note. She read through it again, hoping against hope that she'd only imagined the similarity, but no such luck. Even if the message wasn't verbatim, its meaning was the same.

Hi, Aubrey. Have you missed me? Well, I have good news—I finally have time for you. I promise we'll have fun—or at least I will. See you soon.

The words continued to play like a drumbeat in her head to the point she wanted to scream. She finally gripped the edge of the table hard enough to make her hands ache. It was the best way to stop herself from sliding down onto the floor to curl up in a ball of pure misery. Using every bit of determination she could muster, she pushed past the acid-burn of fear to formulate a plan.

When she could finally draw a full breath, Aubrey carefully refolded the note and stuffed it back into the pink envelope. Then she shoved both it and the box into the padded envelope. Hoping to find a moment of peace, she closed her eyes and offered up a prayer asking God for strength and guidance. As always, putting her trust in Him helped her feel centered and back in control. Finally, she braced her hands on the table and stood, moving slowly to make sure her legs would support her. Proud of her success, she put the padded envelope back in her canvas bag, picked up her purse and headed for the door.

It might have been smarter to call the police, but she didn't want them swarming all over her home. It was her sanctuary, and she was careful whom she let come inside. No, she would go to them and share the news. Finally, after twelve years, her cold case had just turned hot.

Detective Jonah Kelly nodded in response to greetings from several of his coworkers as he made his way through the cluster of desks that formed the heart and soul of the small police department in Elkton, Washington. Under other circumstances, he might have stopped to chat with a few people, but right now it was all he could do to keep moving forward. He'd spent the late morning and early afternoon at the doctor's office followed by one of his twice weekly physical therapy appointments. Translation: he was now in a world of hurt.

The therapist had warned him that he'd pushed too hard

and done too much, but Jonah disagreed. He'd do whatever it took to get both his life and his career back on track. To work out in the field, he needed to regain a lot more mobility in his right leg. Progress was being made, but there was a long way to go. Even a single bullet did a lot of damage to a knee joint.

When he finally made it into the minuscule office they'd assigned him, Jonah closed the door and quit pretending that he could walk without limping. Gritting his teeth, he slowly lowered himself into the desk chair and stretched out his right leg, trying to find a position that didn't hurt. When that didn't pan out, he gave up and settled for one that ached a little less.

Choosing a file at random, Jonah began reading, forcing himself to go slow and not just skim over the information previous investigators had recorded in their reports. He jotted down a few notes, but nothing of consequence. From what he could tell, that seemed to be the nature of working cold case files. Every so often someone would review the file in case a fresh pair of eyes would spot something no one else had seen. It wasn't that the police didn't care about cold cases, but sometimes the evidence simply didn't lead anywhere no matter how much they hoped it would.

An hour later, he got up to get a cup of coffee. It was really more of an excuse to stretch his legs and ensure the right one didn't lock up completely from being in one position too long. After adding two sugars and a heaping spoonful of creamer, he started the slow trek back toward his desk. If he were at home, he could've used heat and then ice to ease the pain. He might have also taken one of the prescription pain pills he allowed himself only on the worst days.

Here at work, the most Jonah could do was a few slow stretches and then try to get lost in the next file in the huge pile of reports left to him by his predecessor. Detective George Swahn had worked the department's cold cases for over two decades. He'd been ready to retire for a while now, but he'd been waiting for the right guy to come along and take his place. When that didn't happen, he'd given up and settled for Jonah. They both knew this wasn't the kind of work Jonah wanted to be doing, but right now he didn't have much choice but to accept a position that was pretty much a desk job.

At least working alone eliminated the possibility of watching another officer bleed out in the street. On the night he'd been shot, Jonah had screamed himself hoarse as he crawled to his dying partner's side. He'd gotten there too late to do anything except pray that God would watch over Gino's widow and their three kids.

That had been two months ago, but the memory of watching Gino die was never far from Jonah's thoughts. At night, he often lay awake for hours trying to find answers to the questions that plagued him from the beginning. How had a simple interview with a witness gone so wrong? And if someone had to die in that alley, why had it been Gino, loving husband and father, instead of Jonah? That was something he'd been asking himself, his therapist, and even God over and over again. Sadly, he was no closer to understanding the why of it all than he'd been when he'd regained consciousness in the hospital.

Heavy footsteps approached, stopping a few feet away. "Hey, Jonah, the desk sergeant is looking for you. Evidently there's an Aubrey Sims downstairs in the lobby, and she's insisting on speaking to you. Something about a weird envelope."

With some effort Jonah shut down his prior train of thought and turned to face Sergeant Tim Decker. The standing joke was that Decker had been part of the original equipment when the precinct was first built. Jonah had never had the courage to ask the man how long he'd been on the job. But based on his wiry gray hair and the deep wrinkles framing his eyes and mouth, the sergeant had a lot of long, hard miles on him.

That said, Decker's mind remained razor sharp, and Jonah wasn't the only detective who consulted him when they needed advice on a case. There wasn't much he hadn't seen or done when it came to law enforcement.

"Did they say what was weird about the envelope?"

"Nope, other than she insisted it was definitely something you needed to see. Seems she made it pretty clear that there was no way she'd leave it with anyone else."

When Decker didn't immediately walk away after delivering the message, Jonah figured the sergeant's own curiosity had kicked in. "It must be one of Detective Swahn's old cases. I'll hunt up the file, and then we'll go see what's up."

It didn't take Jonah long to pull the file. Rather than keep the woman waiting any longer, he decided he could wait to review the details when he found out more about what had brought her to the station today. He and Sergeant Decker left his office and turned in the direction of the elevator in the far corner. The staircase was closer, but everyone knew steps weren't exactly Jonah's best friends these days. Decker quietly adjusted his stride to match Jonah's as they crossed the room. When he pushed the button to summon the elevator, he quietly asked, "You're probably tired of being asked a lot of questions, but are you doing okay?"

It was wrong to react to genuine concern with anger, and the older man certainly deserved better than for Jonah to growl at him. Instead, he waited to answer until they were inside the elevator with the door closed. "It varies. I had physical therapy today, so right now my knee is barking at me."

They both knew Decker wasn't only asking about the state of Jonah's knee, but at least he didn't press the issue. "It'll get better. Those docs work miracles these days. I had a knee replacement last year, and it's amazing how much more I can do these days."

The slow-moving elevator settled on the first floor, one level down from where Jonah's office was located. They started toward the lobby at the front of the building. The desk sergeant looked relieved to see them coming.

"Thanks for coming down, Detective Kelly."

"Anytime, Sergeant. Decker here says an Aubrey Sims asked to see me."

"Yeah, she did." He dropped his voice to a low whisper as he glanced down at the clipboard in front of him. "Just so you know, I recognized her from her previous visits. She used to ask for Detective Swahn, but I guess maybe she'd heard he'd retired. I put her in the first conference room."

Sergeant Decker followed Jonah down the hall. They stopped by the window into the conference room long enough to check out the woman inside. At the moment, her attention was focused on a canvas bag lying on the table, which afforded them an opportunity to study her for a few seconds.

"Do you recognize her?"

Jonah started to shake his head, but then an image popped into his head that changed his mind. He'd worked alongside Detective Swahn the last week before the other man had officially retired. About the third day, they'd spent the morning reviewing cases Swahn thought deserved special attention. They were on their way to lunch when Swahn spotted someone standing on the far side of the lobby.

He'd drawn a sharp breath, his shoulders sagging slightly. In a low voice, he explained his reaction. "No matter how hard we all try, there are cases that won't ever have a satisfactory ending, which means some folks will never find closure. For those of us who work cold cases, that percentage is even higher. My advice is to learn how to let go of the frustration and take satisfaction from the cases you do manage to close."

The older detective gave the young woman a pointed look. "Having said that, there are always going to be some that stick with you and always will. Aubrey Sims over there comes in every few months to see if there's been any progress on her case. I hate—really, really *hate*—having to tell her that nothing's changed. I'm not going to miss this part of the job."

With that depressing memory in mind, Jonah finally answered Decker's question. "Sadly, I'm pretty sure I do."

Then he entered the conference room alone and closed the door.

TWO

Aubrey was already regretting her decision to leave the safety of her house to drive down to the police station. It had seemed like a good plan right up until she found herself waiting alone in a room with a door without a lock. Worse yet, it had a large window right beside the door, which meant anyone out in the hallway could see her. Granted, the vast majority of the people passing by probably worked there, but she still felt exposed, her nerves raw. The tension had her pacing the length of the room rather than sitting down at the table.

She supposed she could simply leave if it all became too much to handle. After all, the desk sergeant had offered to personally deliver the envelope to the new cold case detective. It was tempting to take the man at his word and scurry back to the security of her own home. Unfortunately, the new detective was bound to have a lot of questions about the envelope and its contents, ones that only she could answer. The bottom line was that she could either do that here at the station or wait until after he inevitably showed up at her house.

Preferring to get back home before dark, she decided to wait no more than another five minutes. After that, maybe she would leave and try again tomorrow. The decision was made for her when footsteps came to a stop right outside the room followed by the muffled sound of two men talking. A few seconds later, the door opened just a crack, but no one entered immediately. However, there was an older uniformed officer watching her through the window. When he realized he'd been spotted, he offered her a smile she thought was meant to be reassuring before disappearing from sight.

It seemed a bit odd, but she was more concerned about the man who finally stepped inside the room. After shutting the door, he stopped to close the blinds on the window. Maybe she wasn't the only one who preferred some privacy.

"Ms. Sims?"

"Yes."

His smile was a little less practiced than the other officer's, but it seemed more sincere as a result. "I'm Detective Jonah Kelly. I took over your case from Detective Swahn when he retired. I asked Sergeant Decker to get us some bottled water. I don't know about you, but I always find talking to be thirsty work."

As he spoke, he stepped closer and offered his hand. After she shook it, he retreated to the other side of the table. "He should be back soon, and then we can get started."

She sat across from him and folded her hands in her lap while he set down the file folder he'd brought with him and then took out a small notebook and a pen. The door opened a second later, and the sergeant stepped inside to set two bottles of water on the table. "Is there anything else you need?"

He directed the question at the detective, but he kept

his gaze on Aubrey as he spoke. She shook her head at the same time Detective Kelly answered, "Not right now."

"You've got my number if that changes."

Then he left, quietly closing the door on his way out. As soon as the sergeant was gone, Detective Kelly opened his water and took a quick drink. Aubrey did the same while she struggled to get her chaotic thoughts to settle into some semblance of order.

"So, Ms. Sims, I understand that you wanted to show me something."

Swallowing hard, she pulled the envelope out of the canvas bag and set it on her side of the table. Pointing at his bare hands, she said, "You should wear gloves before you touch it. I wish I had thought to do that myself. Unfortunately by the time I realized what was inside, it was already too late."

At least he didn't question her suggestion. Instead, he pulled a pair of gloves out of his suitcoat pocket and slipped them on. Before surrendering the envelope, she asked, "How familiar are you with my case?"

He looked a bit chagrined as he shot a guilty look at the file on the table. "To be honest, I only recently took over the cold case files from Detective Swahn, so I'm still going through everything. I thought about reviewing your file before coming downstairs, but I didn't want to keep you waiting any longer than necessary."

She hated having to start over from scratch, but maybe it wasn't a bad thing. At least he would be looking at everything with fresh eyes. "Actually, there's not much to tell. Twelve years ago, my friend and I were kidnapped at gunpoint in a parking lot after we got out of a late class. He drugged both of us, so I don't remember anything from then until we woke up chained together in a cabin some-where in the woods. After he decided to only keep one of us, I was found on the side of the road a day later. My friend hasn't been seen since."

By the end of her quick spiel, Detective Kelly definitely had his cop face on. "I'm sorry."

Her answering smile had nothing to do with happiness. "Me, too."

She finally shoved the envelope across the table. If he noticed how badly her hands were shaking, he was kind enough not to comment. "I have my mail delivered to a post office box and usually only pick it up once a week. I have no idea when that envelope actually arrived."

Detective Kelly had started taking notes, so she waited for him to catch up before continuing. "I waited until I got home to open the envelope. That's when I noticed there was no return address. Maybe that should have set off alarms, but it didn't. I'm sorry if I've contaminated the evidence."

"Have you ever gotten anything like this before?"

When she shook her head, he said, "Then there's nothing to apologize for. How were you supposed to know some-thing was wrong?"

She appreciated his effort to reassure her even if it didn't really help. "Regardless, something about it made me un-comfortable."

"Besides the lack of a return address?"

"Yes. At first, I thought maybe my mom or a friend might have ordered a surprise present to be sent directly to me, but it's not my birthday or anything. Besides, a commercial shipment would normally have a printed label."

By that point, she couldn't bear to look at the envelope. Instead, she kept her gaze focused on the man across from her. "There's a small box with a buffalo head nickel inside along with a note addressed to me."

"Does that specific coin hold a special significance?"

She managed a small nod. "It looks like the one they found hidden in my shoe when I was rescued. I figure he put it there because I didn't have any pockets. The note also echoes something my abductor said twelve years ago. Back then, he said he didn't have time to enjoy both of us. He flipped that coin to choose between us. After that, they found me tied to a tree on the side of a road. We've never found out what happened to Marta."

She swallowed hard, her fear a huge wave that threatened to overwhelm her. "Basically, this note says he finally has time for me."

Detective Kelly's hand slammed down hard on the table, his anger clear. He immediately apologized. "Sorry for losing my temper, Ms. Sims. You've been through enough for one day and don't need any more drama. My temper wasn't directed at you but at whoever mailed that envelope."

"It's all right, Detective. I'm pretty upset about this situation myself. So what do we do next? And how long will it take? I'd like to get back home before dark."

He frowned. "Do you have friends or family you can stay with?"

That was the last thing she wanted to do. "I'd rather go home."

"Okay, then." He studied the envelope for several seconds before finally meeting her gaze again. "Right now, I'm trying to decide whether I should open the envelope myself or have the forensics team take over now."

A second later, he nodded. "Yeah, the forensics people should have first crack at it. I'll ask them to give it priority, but I can't make any promises. I'll come to your house when I know what they find."

He checked the time. "I'm guessing that won't be until tomorrow sometime. Is that all right with you?"

She knew that last part was his attempt to let her think she had some control over the situation. While she appreciated his consideration, they both knew he would show up whether she wanted him to or not. Besides, she needed his help.

"I'm a school teacher. I normally get home around four thirty. Any time after that should be fine."

All too ready to be done and out of there, Aubrey picked up her purse and her canvas bag, leaving the envelope on the table. With keys in hand, she rose to her feet. "I'll be going. Thank you for meeting with me on such short notice, Detective Kelly. I appreciate it."

"Any time, but give me a minute before you leave. I'd feel better if Sergeant Decker makes sure you get back home safely."

He pulled out his cell phone and made a quick call. "Sarge, I need you to escort Ms. Sims back to her house. She might appreciate it if you make sure everything is secure when you get there."

When Detective Kelly ended the call, she offered him a small smile. "I'd like to say that's not necessary, but the truth is I'll sleep better if he really has time, that is."

"He's on his way. I'd walk you out to your car myself, but I have to stay with the evidence." Then he held out a business card. "That's my number. Call any time, day or night. Otherwise, I'll see you tomorrow."

"I'll be waiting."

Sergeant Decker walked in a minute later. "You ready to

go, Ms. Sims? I hope it's okay, but I'm going to ride with you while one of our patrol officers follows behind. I'll do a perimeter check as well as check the inside of the house while she stays outside with you. Afterward, she'll bring me back to the station."

Detective Kelly looked happier. "Good thinking, Sergeant. I'll also ask the officers who patrol that area to drive by the house more often until we figure out what's going on."

Aubrey followed Sergeant Decker out to her car. While they waited for the other officer to join them, she couldn't decide if their efforts to provide safe escort back to her house were reassuring or only scared her more knowing they thought it was necessary.

Despite his decision to have the forensics people take charge of the evidence, Jonah was seriously tempted to rip the envelope open right then and there. He knew better: procedures were meant to be followed for good reason. It was important to protect the evidence to ensure the case would hold up if and when it ever came to trial. The last thing anyone wanted to happen was to have the case thrown out of court because someone got careless.

With that in mind, he pulled out his phone and made a quick call. "I need someone from Forensics in the conference room off the lobby ASAP."

While he waited, he skimmed through the case file to familiarize himself with the basic facts. Even the little he read was the stuff of nightmares. No wonder the coin and the note had left Aubrey Sims pale and shaking. He'd only gotten through the initial report when the forensics tech arrived. After she did her thing, Jonah followed her down to the lab.

For the next hour, he hovered as close as he could to the two technicians who were processing the envelope and its contents. He snapped pictures at each step of the way even though the forensics team handled the official documentation of the evidence. At least this way he would have his own photos to use until they finished processing everything.

They finally opened the envelope and gently slid its contents onto the counter. Just as Aubrey had told him, there was a small box about two inches square and a pink envelope, which held a single piece of white paper folded in thirds. The technician carefully removed the lid from the box to reveal a coin nestled on top of a thin layer of cotton. After photographing that much, she unfolded the note and laid it flat next to the box.

Then she stood back to allow Jonah a closer look. The coin didn't tell him much, but his breath caught in his chest as soon as he read the words scrawled across the paper. No wonder Aubrey had been so badly shaken by the contents of the envelope.

The tech gave him a curious look. "From your reaction, I'm guessing there's good reason to be concerned about the young woman who brought this in."

"Yeah, there is." Although Jonah wished he was wrong about that. Sadly, the threat was all too clear, especially after what he'd read in Aubrey's case file.

Leaving the techs to finish their work, Jonah hustled out of the lab as fast as his aching leg would let him. He didn't even try to hide his need to limp as he headed back to his office.

When he sat down at his desk, he did his best to ignore the jagged shards of pain shooting up his leg. His knee clearly wasn't very happy about all the walking and standing Jonah had done over the past couple of hours.

Too bad. Right now he had more important things to worry about, like doing a much deeper dive into the case file to learn everything he could. He started with the investigating officer's report along with all the notes Detective Swahn had added over the years. On his second pass through the jumble of information, Jonah started taking notes, adding his own observations of the potential new evidence.

The details on the case sent chills up Jonah's spine. One thing Aubrey hadn't mentioned was that their captor had used a device to distort his voice. He'd also dressed from head to toe in black, including a mask that hid his face and hair. Those things accounted for why Aubrey couldn't give any useful description of the man who had abducted the two women.

The few things she did remember clearly were the stuff of nightmares. Like how the kidnapper had sounded almost gleeful when he informed the two women that he wouldn't have time to enjoy both of them. No doubt he got off on their terror. Worse yet, they had to watch as he flipped a coin to determine which one would stay and who would get a reprieve. Marta had never been heard from again, but the next day Aubrey had been found beside a rural highway near the Cascades. She'd been groggy but otherwise unharmed, at least physically. The only real evidence they'd found was the coin—a buffalo head nickel.

Jonah studied the picture of the coin in the file and compared it to his photo of the one down in the forensics lab.

They were identical in style; the only significant difference was the year they'd been minted. According to the file, the description of the coin had never been released to the public. Unless Aubrey or possibly someone close to her had let it slip, only the kidnapper would've known what kind of coin he'd used.

Finally, Jonah reviewed Aubrey's original description of what her captor had said in the cabin and compared it to the note that had accompanied the coin. There was no doubt that he'd be coming for Aubrey, and soon.

Jonah picked up his phone and dialed his boss's number. "Captain, we've got a problem."

THREE

The next afternoon, it was a relief to walk through the front door and kick off her shoes. The day had been a rough one, and Aubrey was tired. As promised, Sergeant Decker had checked out her house inside and out yesterday. Aubrey had appreciated his efforts, but she hadn't been able to relax enough to actually sleep well. It had been all she could do to drag herself out of bed and get to work on time.

At least there, she'd been able to put her worries on the back burner and focus on her students. No matter what was going on in her own life, she would do whatever it took to prepare them to move on to fourth grade in the fall. After they boarded the buses for home, she'd rushed through getting organized for the next day and then headed back home.

It was tempting to kick back and relax, but unfortunately her day was far from over. Detective Kelly had texted to remind her he'd be stopping by. Rather than sit and stare at the door while waiting for him to arrive, she fixed herself a glass of iced tea and sat down at the dining room table to pay a few bills. Once those were taken care of, she decided to review the current balances in her three bank accounts. Even after paying the bills, there was plenty in her checking account to cover her expenses for the two next months. Her regular savings account was slightly below her comfort zone. But barring unforeseen circumstances, it should be back up to normal after her next paycheck.

That left her secret account, the one she never mentioned to anyone, especially her parents. After studying the bottom line, she did a few calculations. Sadly, it would take her at least two months to accrue enough money to hire another private investigator. The police had never been able to find out what had happened to Marta, but Aubrey had kept hoping another trained professional could. Of course, with the arrival of the coin and the note, maybe all of that would change.

Scary as it all was, she hoped so.

Over the past twelve years, she'd paid out a lot of money in the hope that someone would miraculously discover something that would blow the case wide open. That had yet to happen, so she had kept all knowledge of the investigations to herself and for good reason. For starters, Detective Swahn had expressed considerable doubt that a private investigator would be able to ferret out any information that the police had missed. She truly believed that wasn't his ego talking, that he was giving her what he thought was good advice. Regardless, she'd never forgive herself if she didn't make every possible effort to find answers. At least he'd never once questioned her determination to make sure the police kept looking for Marta.

The biggest reason for the secrecy regarding her efforts to keep the investigation moving forward had more to do with opinions expressed by Aubrey's parents and most of her friends. They stood united behind the idea that it was well past time for Aubrey to put the kidnapping behind her and get on with her life. Even the ones who'd known

Marta personally believed whatever had happened to her was tragic but hardly Aubrey's fault.

Her parents had insisted Aubrey see a therapist when she couldn't simply let it all go. In his opinion, she was developing an unhealthy fixation. She'd quickly quit going to him when it became obvious he never really listened to her. Instead, he simply parroted everything her parents had already told her—that nothing good would come from her insistence on wanting answers.

They were wrong, and so was he.

To this day, she was as puzzled by their attitudes as they were by hers. Just how was she supposed to forget the two days she been held captive? After all, those forty-eight hours and everything that had occurred afterward had changed her life on a fundamental level. With a flip of a coin, the person Aubrey had been when she and Marta walked out of class that night had ceased to exist. She understood why her parents wanted that girl back, but that was never going to happen.

Besides, did they have no sympathy for Marta's family? Mr. and Mrs. Pyne would give anything, do anything, to find out what had happened to their daughter. She prayed that Detective Kelly would somehow make that happen.

Speaking of him, she had a phone call to make before he actually arrived. He might not appreciate her reaching out to his predecessor, but that wasn't going to stop her. After finding Detective Swahn in her contacts, she dialed his home phone number. He'd given it to her the last time they'd spoken at the police station, just in case. He wasn't clear in case of what exactly, but she'd appreciated the gesture. When he didn't immediately answer, she debated whether to stay on the line long enough to leave a message or if she should simply hang up. The decision was made for her when his voice finally came on the line.

"Ms. Sims, sorry to keep you waiting. I'm mowing the lawn and didn't hear it ringing at first. What can I do for you?"

She managed a small laugh. "No need to start being formal now that you're retired. You've always called me Aubrey, Detective Swahn."

"Fine, Aubrey. How can I help?"

That was the question, wasn't it? "I apologize for bothering you, and maybe I shouldn't be asking this, but I was wondering what you could tell me about Detective Kelly."

She tried to sound calm, as if she were asking the question more out of curiosity than real concern. However, something in her voice must have alerted Detective Swahn that something was going on. "What's happened, Aubrey?"

She gave him the basics. "I received an anonymous envelope with a buffalo head nickel and a note inside. I'm pretty sure it's from the kidnapper. I turned it over to Detective Kelly yesterday, and he's stopping by this evening to give me an update on what the forensics people found."

After a heavy silence, the detective sighed. "I'm so sorry, Aubrey. You must be scared, but you did the right thing by taking it directly to Jonah. He's a good detective, and you can trust him. I wish there was something I could do to help."

"You already have just by vouching for him." She forced a cheerier note into her voice. "Now I should let you get back to your chores. That grass won't mow itself."

"So true. But one more thing before I go, Aubrey. Tell Jonah to call me if I can do anything to help."

She pointed out the obvious. "You're retired."

"I know, but tell him anyway."

"I will."

She hung up and put her bank statements back in the file cabinet and then started working on her lesson plans for the remaining days of school. She was just finishing up when the doorbell rang. She closed the file on her laptop and then got up to peek out the front window. There was an unfamiliar black sedan parked in the driveway. Next, she checked the security feed on her phone app to verify it was Detective Kelly standing on her porch. He was dressed much as he had been yesterday although his suit looked a bit rumpled, and he'd removed his tie at some point. Evidently she wasn't the only one who'd put in a lot of long hours already, and the day wasn't over yet.

Aubrey took a deep breath and forced herself to unlock the door. When she finally swung it open, Detective Kelly had retreated to the far edge of the porch, probably trying not to crowd her. "I hope I didn't catch you in the middle of dinner."

"Not at all. I was just finishing up my lesson plans for tomorrow."

"Well, hopefully I won't take up too much of your time." He studied her and then asked, "Would you feel more comfortable if we talk out here on your porch?"

She looked up and down the street and was relieved to see that several of her neighbors were out and about. Feeling slightly more in control of the situation, she stepped outside. At the same time, Detective Kelly sat in one of the two Adirondack chairs that flanked a small wicker table. The roomy porch was one of her favorite features on her small bungalow. She liked to relax out there and watch the bees buzz around the riot of flowers in her front yard.

Right now, though, she doubted anything would soothe her nerves.

The detective sat quietly, as if he'd give her all the time she needed to get settled. When she finally got herself situated, he picked up a file he'd left lying on the table and briefly studied it before speaking. "I've reviewed the details of your case. I wanted to make sure I was up-to-date on everything that has happened since the beginning. I know it probably doesn't help, but it's clear that your case has always been important to Detective Swahn. He was really frustrated that he could never find answers for you."

She bit her lower lip and tried to decide if she should mention she had just spoken with the other detective. Considering there was likely a good chance that Detective Kelly might consult with his predecessor at some point, it was probably better to come clean from the get-go. "I should probably confess that I just got off the phone with him a little while ago. He gave me his number the last time we spoke. He wanted me to have it in case I ever I had questions."

Detective Kelly surprised her by grinning. "So you were checking up on me?"

At least he wasn't angry. "Yeah, pretty much. He said good things about you and that you could call him about my case if there's anything he could do to help."

"I will probably reach out to George at some point. He knows more about not only your case, but all of the others I inherited from him. He went over as many of them with me as we had time for before he left. I really appreciated all the good advice he gave me."

"He's always been very kind to me. I was truly sorry to

hear he was retiring, which probably sounds pretty self-ish of me. I hope he has some fun adventures planned."

"From what he told me, George plans to do a lot of fishing." He grinned a little. "At least after he gets caught up on the long list of chores his wife had lined up for him. He also grumbled something about an Alaskan cruise she booked for later this summer."

She could picture the dour detective being grumpy about that, but she'd always suspected he was a marshmallow inside. "I bet he'll have a great time despite himself."

"I hope so. After being on the force for so long, the man deserves to have a little fun. So does his wife."

Evidently the pleasantries were now over, because he turned to face her more directly. From the way his brows were riding low over those bright blue eyes, whatever he was about to say wasn't going to be easy to hear.

"So, let's go over what we know so far."

He handed her a piece of paper with an enlarged picture of the front and back of the coin that had been in the envelope. After she studied the photo closely, he handed her a second one. "That first one is the coin you received yesterday. I got the second picture from your case file. Presumably, it's the coin the kidnapper used to decide which of you he would release."

She shuddered at the memory of that moment. "So we're dealing with two different coins. I admit I was wondering if the police had lost track of the original one somehow. Not that I think they're normally careless about such things, but it has been twelve years. No offense, but sometimes things happen."

He waved off her apology. "Don't worry about it. To be honest I wondered about that myself. Earlier today, I personally verified the original coin is still in our evidence lockup. The two coins do look a lot alike, but they were minted in different years. The original one from twelve years ago was minted in 1925, while the one you got yesterday is from 1932."

She handed back the photos. "I'll take your word for it. I haven't seen that coin in twelve years. It was taken into evidence along with all of my clothes at the hospital."

The truth was, though, the memory of that coin still haunted her dreams.

Next, the detective handed her a photocopy of the note. "I've reviewed your statements from twelve years ago. I wish I could tell you that your memory was faulty and that the wording in the note isn't remarkably similar to what you reported at the time, but I can't. I've gone over everything with my captain and one of the original investigating officers. It's our opinion that whoever sent you that note clearly had insider knowledge. He's either the actual kidnapper or he was there."

He wasn't telling her anything she hadn't already suspected. But there was a big difference between mere suspicion and hearing a trained professional state it as fact. Aubrey wanted to deny the reality of the situation, but she couldn't tear her eyes away from the words on the page. At first glance, they were clear, but then they seemed to melt and swirl on the paper. Black spots danced in her eyes as she struggled to deny the meaning of what she'd read. She kept blinking, hoping to clear her vision.

When that didn't work, she tried to give the paper back, to put some distance between herself and the terror that threatened to overwhelm her. Why would this be happening after all these years? Granted, she'd always hoped to find out the truth about what had happened to Marta, but she'd never expected to get sucked back into the nightmare herself.

Why did he finally have time for Aubrey? There was no way to know. As the truth of the situation slowly sank in, she rose to her feet and struggled to speak to the detective. To tell him to leave and take the threat with him. When she couldn't manage even that much, going into full retreat was her only option. But before she could find the way back inside the house, a wave of pure darkness washed over her and sent Aubrey plunging toward the ground.

FOUR

Jonah lunged forward to catch Aubrey before she hit the ground. His knee protested the additional weight he put on it as he lifted her back up to the chair. She was already coming around, which was a good thing. He remained next to her, his hand resting on her shoulder with enough pressure to make sure she kept her head down between her knees. She'd already been skittish around him. The last thing he wanted to do was crowd her so much that she'd panic again.

In a matter of seconds, she waved him off. "I'm fine."

No, she wasn't; not really. Rather than argue the point, he asked, "Will you be all right here while I get you some water to drink? I promise I will go in and come right back out." He took a small step back and held up his phone. "Unless you'd rather I call the EMTs so they can check you over."

She immediately shook her head. "There's no need. I'll be fine, but water would be nice. The glasses are in the cabinet above and to the left of the sink. The fridge has a built-in ice and water dispenser on the door. Fix yourself some, too, if you'd like."

Still he hesitated but finally decided a quick trip inside would be okay if she was thinking clearly enough to play hostess. "I'll be right back."

Hustling as fast as he could, he ducked inside and headed for the galley-style kitchen beyond the dining area to his right. A cozy living room was on his left with another doorway on the far end that probably led to the bedrooms. Once in the kitchen, he filled two glasses halfway with ice and topped them off with water. He also grabbed some cookies from a glass jar on the counter. A bit of sugar would probably do her some good.

Aubrey's coloring had improved by the time he returned with their drinks. He set his drink and the cookies on the table. Then he wrapped his hand around hers to support her glass until he was sure she had a solid grip on it. "Drink a little of that and then eat a cookie."

She took several sips and then offered him a tenuous smile. "Thank you. That helps."

"I'm not sure you should be thanking me for anything since it's my fault you almost took a header." Jonah was pretty sure his smile was nearly as shaky as hers. He returned to his seat and took out his spiral notebook to take notes. "I'm sorry about that. I should've found a better way to let you know what we're thinking."

"No apologies necessary, Detective Kelly, although I'll admit all of this has hit me hard." She reached for one of the cookies before continuing. "I've always hoped something would break loose on the case. Twelve years is a long time to wait for answers."

As far as he could tell, they didn't actually have any answers, only more questions. Jonah considered his next words carefully. "Like I said, I'm operating under the assumption that whoever wrote that note is the same man who abducted you and Ms. Pyne twelve years ago. At the very least, it would have to be him or else someone who had firsthand knowledge of the original case."

Jonah paused to give her a chance to process that much before continuing. When she nodded, he picked up where he'd left off. "I wish I could say I've uncovered something everyone else missed in the initial investigation, but I haven't. I have started searching our database for other incidents with similar details in the intervening years. Basically, cases involving young women, a remote cabin, black clothing, a coin, etc."

He stared off into the distance and ran his fingers through his hair in frustration. "So far, I haven't found any in our general area that meet those criteria, but I'll widen the search as I have time. Considering the almost total lack of forensic evidence from the original incident and the fact your friend has never been found, it seems unlikely your abduction was the first time the guy did something like this. He made sure there was nothing that would lead us back to him, which speaks of practice."

Aubrey sighed. "I've always hoped he'd spontaneously stopped."

"Sadly, that's highly unlikely. This kind of compulsion usually builds over time to the point it picks up speed. If he did stop for a time, there could have been some outside force at play. For example, he might have served time for an unrelated crime. Recuperating from a severe injury or even an illness might also be possibilities. Regardless, it appears he's back now, even if the note and the coin don't give us much of a starting point."

Aubrey studied him a few seconds and bit her lower lip, probably trying to decide whether she should tell him something. He decided to wait her out rather than trying to force the issue. Finally, she drew a sharp breath and spoke in a rush. "I have other files that you can review."

That comment had him sitting upright again. "What kind of files?"

"Detective Swahn told me what I wanted to do was a bad idea. He knew about the first time, but not the others. For sure my parents would have a fit if they found out, but I had to do something."

"I'm sorry, but I'm not following."

Her chin took on a stubborn tilt as if she was feeling a bit defensive. "Over the years, I've hired various private investigators to look into the case. Most did a cursory review and told me there wasn't any reason to continue. I think they felt guilty taking more of my money when they didn't turn up any promising leads."

Some detectives didn't much appreciate having civilians poking their noses into police business, but Jonah couldn't blame Aubrey for resorting to extreme measures to find answers. His trip into the house had been brief, but he hadn't missed seeing the multiple locks on the front door or the baseball bat sitting within easy reach. There was also a container of pepper spray on the lamp table next to the sofa. She might have survived the abduction, but it had profoundly changed the trajectory of her life.

"Did these investigators learn anything useful at all?"

She sighed. "If they had, I would've immediately taken the information to Detective Swahn. I'll understand if you don't want to bother looking through the reports, but I thought you should know about them."

He wasn't about to ignore another source of information. "Is it all right if I copy them and return the originals?"

"There's no need. You can take my hard copies with you. I have it all backed up on both my laptop and a flash drive."

"Great. I'll take the files with me when I leave. I'll read

through them as soon as I can and let you know if I find something useful."

"I would appreciate that. I've read them all, of course, but a trained eye might see something I missed."

It was time to ask some difficult questions. Hopefully, they wouldn't send her into another tailspin. "I have to be honest with you, Ms. Sims. This guy made a pretty bold first move sending you the note and the coin. He has to suspect you would call us. Our involvement would only complicate any plans he might have."

Just that quickly, she latched on to the arms of her chair as she looked up and down the street with wide, panicky eyes. "Maybe it wasn't the first thing he did."

Jonah sat up straighter and scanned the surrounding neighborhood. "Why would you say that?"

"I know this might sound strange, but recently I've had the strangest feeling that I'm being watched. Not all the time, but enough that I've noticed."

She closed her eyes and then opened them again as she turned to meet Jonah's gaze. "I haven't seen anyone, you understand. It's more like a weird feeling that someone is watching the house or staring at me as I load the bags into my car at the grocery store."

"Why didn't you call Detective Swahn or me to let us know?"

"Because in the absence of any kind of proof, it would sound like I'm just being paranoid." She shifted her eyes away from him, "And I might know who it was. If I'm right, they would never hurt me. I believe that."

By that point, Jonah was beyond frustrated with her half answers. "What exactly are we talking about here, Ms. Sims? Because from where I'm sitting, it sure sounds as if someone has been stalking you. If there's any chance it's same the person who sent the note, then his behavior has escalated big-time."

Her dark eyes filled with tears that trickled down her cheek. "Marta became engaged shortly before we were abducted, and her fiancé took her disappearance understandably hard. I'm sure Ross doesn't blame me for what happened, not really. Regardless, I'm not sure he's ever forgiven me for being the one who was set free."

Seriously? Did the jerk not realize that Aubrey was as much a victim as Marta had been, even if they'd suffered very different fates? The burden of guilt Aubrey carried for just being alive took its toll over time and was enough to break some people. Jonah knew that for a fact. After all, he'd learned the hard way exactly what it was like to live with the crippling guilt that came from surviving when your best friend didn't.

He fought the unexpected urge to wrap his arms around Aubrey's slender shoulders and offer whatever comfort she would accept from him. It would be unprofessional on his part, and he needed to maintain an emotional distance for his own sake. That wasn't going to be easy when something about her brought out every protective instinct he had. He flipped through his notebook until he found the guy's name. "To be clear, are we talking about Ross Easton?"

She nodded as she swiped the tears away with the back of her hand. "Yes, but I can't believe that he sent that note. Ross would never torment me like that. Besides, he wouldn't have known about the coin. The police insisted I not share that particular information with anyone. That was especially true after Marta's parents offered a reward for any information that resulted in the return of their daughter. The investigating officers said it was very important that only the kidnapper, the police and I knew what kind of coin he'd used. Keeping it secret would help them sort through any calls that came in on the tip line."

"So, no one outside of you and the investigating officers knew it was a buffalo head nickel?"

"I can't swear to that, but I never even told my parents."

"What about the person who spotted you tied to that tree and called the police?"

Aubrey shook her head. "No, I don't think he would've seen it. The coin was still stuck under the insole in my tennis shoe when the police turned all of my clothes over to your forensics people. They were the ones who found it."

Jonah made a mental note to check the evidence logs to see if anyone had shown any unusual interest in the evidence related to Aubrey's case. The problem was that after twelve years, there were any number of people who had worked on the case. It had started with the patrol officers who had responded to the 911 call when Aubrey had been found, then there was the detective who handled the initial investigation, and so on, until it had eventually been turned over to George Swahn. It was always possible someone had slipped up and mentioned the coin to the wrong person and might not even remember doing it.

"Let's get back to this sensation of someone watching you. Is there anyone else other than this Ross Easton guy who might do something like that?"

She fidgeted in her seat and delayed responding to the question until after she ate another cookie. Finally, Aubrey spoke in a soft whisper. "I don't want to cause any problems for them."

This time he couldn't control his temper. How was he

supposed to help the woman if she held back crucial information? No longer able to sit still, he stood and leaned against the porch railing far enough away to avoid hovering over her. "Aubrey, don't play games with me. I need names."

She slapped her hand over her mouth and looked horrified. "Did I actually say that aloud?"

"Yes, you did, so that cat is out of the bag. Tell me what you're thinking."

"Fine, but I meant what I said. I would really prefer you not bother them with this. They've been through too much already."

"Who has been through too much?"

Although Jonah figured he already knew. Crimes like this one often affected a surprising number of people, just like a stone dropped into still water caused an ever widening series of ripples. Logically speaking, Marta's parents would have been right near the epicenter of the event.

Aubrey's next words confirmed his suspicions. "Mr. and Mrs. Pyne are good people, but they resented that I was the one who got to come home. Marta's disappearance obviously tore a huge hole in their hearts. I understand that, and I continue to pray that they somehow can find some peace in their lives."

That was admirable of her, but he still needed to know what he was dealing with here. "So I take it they've caused you problems in the past."

"Nothing I couldn't handle."

His gut reaction told him that was an out-and-out lie. Whatever they'd done had hurt this woman deeply. She might have found a way to cope with their antics, but she hadn't escaped unscathed.

"I need details."

Aubrey crossed her arms over her chest and shook her head. "No. Besides, I haven't spoken to them in ages. Leave them alone."

Jonah wasn't in the habit of taking orders from civilians and wouldn't start now. Still, the change in her demeanor was interesting to see. A few minutes ago, she'd looked like a stiff breeze would send her tumbling across the yard, but her sympathy for the Pynes had her ready to do battle.

He tried again, this time with a softer approach. "I appreciate your concern for them, but I can't let you tie my hands like this. Tell me what they did. If it's all in the past, then there may be no need for me to ask them about it."

After letting her digest that much, he leaned forward. "But you should know that I will be speaking with everyone who was connected to the case twelve years ago."

When she started to protest, he held up his hand to ward off her next argument. "Yes, I've already reviewed the original statements. That's not the same as hearing it firsthand. I'll be talking to your parents tomorrow."

Her dark eyes flashed hot with anger. "Thanks for the warning. You should know that they will likely refuse to talk to you. I'm sure in your line of work you learn pretty quickly that people handle these situations in vastly different ways. My mom and dad did everything they could to shield me from anything having to do with my case. They didn't want me talking about it to the press, the police, or even them. My mom's attitude was that if we simply quit focusing on what happened, the sooner everything would get back to normal."

She stared into the distance and softly added, "As if it could ever be that easy."

Once again looking haunted by her memories, Aubrey glanced at Jonah before turning her attention to the huge flower bed in her small front yard. "But back to Mr. and Mrs. Pyne—they couldn't handle seeing me patch the pieces of my life back together. It was as if they thought we should all put everything on hold until Marta finally got to come home."

Jonah wasn't surprised. "Time probably has remained frozen for them. In my experience, families have a hard time doing anything beyond watching and waiting for their loved one to walk through the front door again. Nothing else matters and giving up isn't an option."

"I know." She fell silent again for several seconds. "Anyway, I took a semester off from college to recuperate, but then I went back to finish my teaching degree. I couldn't simply sit around and do nothing forever, especially with my parents doing their best to pretend nothing had ever happened at all. At first, I stopped by periodically to check on the Pynes, but it got harder to face them as time went on. Mr. Pyne did his best to be polite, but it was more difficult for his wife to be around me. Finally, he quietly asked me not to come around anymore. To be honest, that was a huge relief."

He jotted down a few notes as he spoke. "I'm guessing that was probably true for them, as well. While your intentions were good, it was a constant reminder of all that they lost. Regardless, you shouldn't feel guilty about no longer visiting them."

She stood and stepped down off the porch. Trying not to crowd her, he followed along as she began systematically deadheading the flowering bushes next to the sidewalk. After a bit, he prodded her into finishing the story. "What happened next?"

"Eventually, I got a job teaching. That's when I bought this house using some money my grandmother left me. I love my parents, but by that point I really needed my own space. While they never liked to talk about what happened, somewhere along the line they turned into… I think the term is 'helicopter parents.' Seriously, if I was five minutes late getting home from work, you would've thought I'd committed a major crime. For sure, they didn't want me to leave the house except to work."

She tossed the dead flowers in a pile and went back to work. "When I moved here, I could finally breathe again, like life had taken a big step back toward normal. A short time later, I met a nice guy at church, and we started dating. I don't know how the Pynes found out, but Mrs. Pyne showed up on my doorstep and demanded to know why I got to have a life when Marta didn't. It would've been one thing if she had limited it to me, but she went after the guy as well. Needless to say, that relationship was over before it even really got started."

"Have they ever done anything like that again?"

Her cheeks flushed a bit pink. "Once. After that, I pretty much gave up dating."

Jonah had to forcibly unclench his fists. He understood the Pynes had been hurting. Probably still were, but that didn't mean their behavior was any kind of okay. Aubrey added her latest collection of dead flowers to the pile and dusted off her hands. "Is there anything else you need to know?"

Her tone made it clear that she thought he'd already poked around in her past enough for one day. "Not right now. If you notice a bigger than normal police presence in your neighborhood, I've asked the patrol officers in this area to do more frequent drives past your home. I've also told my captain that we really need someone detailed to watch your back twenty-four seven. He agreed to make the request but said the budget is tight, so it's unlikely to be okayed unless the threat becomes more specific."

She looked resigned, if not particularly happy about that possibility. "I don't want you to think I'm not appreciative, but is that kind of surveillance really necessary?"

"That we'd even consider the possibility is a sign that we're taking this threat seriously. I would suggest you do the same. Use extra care when you go anywhere. Park near lights if you have to go out at night. Call 911 if anything happens or doesn't look right. Better yet, go stay with your parents so you're not alone."

"That's not going to happen. I fought too long to regain my independence." Then she shivered even standing in the direct sun. "That said, I don't like living scared and jumping at shadows."

"No one does." He handed her another of his business cards. "This is my direct line. Call any time, day or night."

"Thank you." Aubrey studied it for several seconds and stuck it in her pocket. "Before we forget, I'll go get those files for you."

He watched her walk away, sensing that she wouldn't appreciate him following her inside. She was back surprisingly fast, which sadly meant she kept the files close by at all times. As she handed them over, Aubrey mustered up a small smile. "Don't think I'm not grateful for your concern, Detective Kelly. It's just this has stirred up a lot of bad memories."

"It's all right. I know this is difficult. I'll be in touch." He took a step back and added, "And I meant what I said. Call if anything comes up."

"I will."

As he set the box of files in the trunk of his car, he couldn't help but notice how quickly she'd hustled to get back inside. The door was already closed, and no doubt all the locks firmly back in place. All in all, it didn't sound as if those memories she'd mentioned had ever been laid to rest, which was too bad. In a perfect world, a woman like Aubrey Sims deserved a happy life, maybe with that nice guy she mentioned earlier, along with a couple of kids. But instead, the shadows of the past had forced her to take shelter in that tiny house behind locked doors and drawn shades.

He supposed it could be worse. After all, she did get out to run errands and held down a good job. She'd also mentioned church, so maybe she found strength and solace there. He hoped so, because the ghost from her past had raised its ugly head again. Feeling frustrated, he slammed the trunk lid closed with more force than necessary. After one more look up and down the street, he headed back to the office to update the captain on what he'd learned and maybe review the files Aubrey had given him. Tomorrow morning he'd start interviewing the other people connected to the case.

Meanwhile, he offered up a silent prayer that he wouldn't fail Aubrey Sims like he had Gino. Hopefully, this time God would be listening.

FIVE

Aubrey checked her appearance in the mirror before picking up her purse and keys to leave. She didn't have to be at work for another hour, but she preferred to get there a little earlier than usual this time of year. As she stepped out onto the porch, her phone rang. It was tempting to simply ignore it, especially when she saw her mother's name on the screen. It didn't take a genius to know why she was calling.

"Mom, I'm just leaving for work, so I can't really talk now. I'll call you when I get home this afternoon."

She was almost breathless from trying to bulldoze over whatever her mother was saying even though she knew resistance was futile. Her mother was nothing if not stubborn. Surrendering to the inevitable, Aubrey sat down in the closest chair and prepared to listen to the tirade that was coming. "Sorry, Mom, I didn't hear what you were saying."

"That's because you were trying to talk over me, which is nothing short of rude."

"Sorry." Though she really wasn't. "What's up?"

"There is a detective on my front porch demanding to talk to us. What have you done now?"

Aubrey pinched the bridge of her nose and closed her eyes. "I haven't done anything, Mom. And I'm sure Detective Kelly will happily explain the situation if you would simply talk to him."

Her mother's voice jumped up an octave. "Have you been pestering the police again about things we all know are better left in the past?"

"No, but something has happened regarding the case. I did ask Detective Kelly not to bother you and Dad, but he recently took over Detective Swahn's workload. Since the case is new to him, he plans to talk to everyone concerned. Now, I really need to leave for work."

"This fixation is not healthy for you, Aubrey. Perhaps it's time for you to see Dr. Wilcox again."

She tried to head her mother off at the pass. "I've already made it clear that's never going to happen. I can't stop you from talking to Dr. Wilcox about your own issues, but leave me out of it. I have to hang up now. Go talk to Detective Kelly. I'm sure it won't take long."

Then she made good on her threat and disconnected the call with her mother still babbling on the other end of the line. At least the good detective couldn't say he hadn't been warned about how her parents would react to him showing up on their doorstep. No doubt she'd be hearing from one or both of her parents later after she got home from work.

Most likely she'd hear from the detective as well. For some reason that thought wasn't nearly as upsetting as the idea of being lectured by her folks for the umpteenth time on how she should simply forget the past. Detective Kelly might have not appreciated her efforts to shield the Pynes and her folks from the current situation, but at least he'd never once questioned why she still needed answers after all this time.

Under other circumstances, she might've even found

him attractive, but those intelligent blue eyes saw way too much. There was a watchfulness about Jonah Kelly, as if he could see right through to the heart of her fears and insecurities. She worked hard to present a facade to the world that she was strong and whole, not the patched-together mess that she could be at times. The last thing she wanted was a man who saw her as weak or needy.

At least the drive to work was uneventful. Once there, she did her best to shake off her problems and focus on her job. She refused to carry that darkness into the school building with her. The children under her care deserved better.

"You're here bright and early."

She didn't quite contain a squeak of fear at the sound of a man's voice coming from right behind her. It was a huge relief that she recognized who it was before she did something foolish like taking off running for the front door of the building. Pasting on a bright smile, she turned to face her boss. Lyle Peale had taken over as principal of the elementary school the previous school year. He was well liked by the staff as well as the students and their families. Her pulse began to slow down as she greeted him. "Sorry, I didn't see you. Good morning."

He smiled at her. "I didn't mean to startle you. I was just saying that you're here bright and early this morning."

She fell into step with him as they made their way toward the building. "There are a few things I want to get done before the munchkins arrive. You know how it is this time of year. The last few days of school fly by so fast that it's almost impossible to get everything finished before we wave goodbye to the kids for the summer."

"So true. Sadly, my to-do list seems to get longer every

day." He reached around her to open the door to the building. "Do you have big plans for the summer?"

"Nothing special. I have some projects lined up to do around my house. A couple of rooms need to be painted, and I love working out in the yard."

"Well, I hope you take time to relax a little. Personally, I'm planning to get away for a while, maybe driving along the Oregon coast without any particular itinerary."

"Sounds like fun. It's been a long time since I've been down there, but I remember how beautiful it was."

In fact, she'd barely left town in the past twelve years, but he didn't need to know about that. It would only bring up questions she didn't want to answer.

Lyle headed toward the main office where the school secretary immediately stood up with a handful of phone messages in her hand. "Well, looks like I'm needed. Have a great day, Aubrey."

"You, too."

Her classroom was at the far end of the building. Other staff members called out greetings on her way down the hall. She smiled and waved back, stopping to confer with the other third grade teacher about the end-of-the-year activities they had planned. By the time she reached her classroom, her mood was much improved, as if she'd left her worries back out in the parking lot. They'd be waiting for her when she left work, but for now she had happier things to think about.

Hours later Aubrey left the building with a couple of friends, which saved her from having to walk out to the parking lot by herself. Detective Kelly would be so proud of her for taking the precautions he'd suggested. Little did he know that she almost always made sure she wasn't alone when she left work. After all, she and Marta had been grabbed as they headed to the parking lot after class. A person didn't forget something like that.

Once in her car, she gave in and did something that she'd been dreading all day. She checked her phone. Just as she'd expected, both her mother and father had left voice mails demanding she return their calls immediately, even though they knew she was at work. When that had failed, they'd resorted to long angry text messages. She groaned after skimming their content.

Not only did they want to talk about what was going on, they were coming to her house to do so in person. Great, just what she needed. Worse yet, if she didn't get a move on, they would already be there waiting for her. It would be nice if they would at least give her a chance to unwind and maybe even eat a little dinner before they started in on her. Not that she'd be able to actually relax knowing they were on their way, but it was the principle of the thing.

Surrendering to the inevitable, she drove the short distance to her house. It was a relief that her parents' car was nowhere in sight. Instead, there was a certain black sedan parked on the street in front of her house, and its owner had made himself comfortable on her front porch. She wondered how long Detective Kelly been waiting and why he was there at all.

He stood as soon as she pulled into the driveway and then hustled to help her carry in the pile of papers and other stuff she'd brought home to work on that evening. As he followed her back toward the porch, she said, "Detective, I thought you were going to call."

"I was in the neighborhood and thought I'd stop by to

see how you were doing." He looked past her toward the car slowing to pull into her driveway. "I also wanted to warn you how things went when I talked to your folks this morning. I know your mother called you to demand answers before she'd even let me inside the house."

Aubrey actually laughed at that. "Yeah, she wasn't happy, especially when I hung up on her because I had to get to work. If she took her anger out on you, I'm sorry."

He managed a small smile. "I've been in tougher situations and survived."

As they talked, she unlocked the door and led the way inside. "Can I fix you a glass of iced tea or a can of pop? I think I have cola and root beer."

"Iced tea sounds good. Should I let your parents in?"

She pretended to think it over as she poured four glasses of tea and tossed a few cookies on a plate and set them all on the dining room table. That was going to be pretty much her limit on playing hostess, especially since none of her guests had actually been invited. "I suppose there's no getting around it. If I don't open the door, they'll start banging on it."

Jonah followed her to the door, standing slightly behind her as if providing backup in case it was needed. She took a deep breath before turning the doorknob. "Brace yourself, Detective."

Just as Aubrey had expected, her mother had her fist raised to start pounding on the door. It was hard not to laugh when she almost fell across the threshold as Aubrey opened the door. "Mom, Dad, what a pleasant surprise."

Her companion made an odd noise like he was trying to cover up a laugh with a fake cough. At least someone was amused by the current situation. Her mother sailed into the room as if she owned the place, while her father shot her an apologetic look on his way past.

"Why don't we all have a seat at the table?"

Rather than follow the simple directive, her mom stopped to glare at Detective Kelly. "What are you doing here? I told you to stay away from our daughter."

He shrugged. "That's not your decision to make. I have a job to do, and I will see it done."

Jonah sauntered over to the table and politely pulled out a chair for Aubrey before settling into the one next to her. Maybe he assumed her father would do the same for his wife, or else he'd decided that her mother's behavior didn't deserve his best manners. After a second, her mother huffed and pointed toward the door. "Detective, we're here to have a discussion with Aubrey, a *private* discussion. And in case you didn't get the hint, you're not welcome here."

Aubrey sincerely hoped that Detective Kelly never aimed that kind of smile in her direction. He calmly met her mother's gaze as he reached for a cookie. "I'm here for the same reason, Mrs. Sims. I'm not leaving until I have a chance to review a few things with your daughter."

His voice remained calm even as his expression turned harsh. "And as I explained this morning, my investigation into the events of the past couple of days, as well as what happened twelve years ago, will continue—with or without your approval or cooperation."

Her father joined the conversation. "Why can't you understand that we don't want the case reopened?"

Aubrey wasn't going to sit on the sidelines and let the other three people in the room debate the issue. "Mom, Dad, stop this right now. The case isn't being reopened. It was never closed in the first place."

She turned to face Jonah. "Correct me if I'm wrong, Detective Kelly, but my understanding is that the file will never be closed until whoever kidnapped me and Marta that night has been brought to justice."

Detective Kelly backed her play. "That's correct, Ms. Sims. Cold cases may go inactive. However, they are all reviewed periodically to see if perhaps new forensic techniques are available or if some new evidence has come to light."

Her parents exchanged unhappy looks before her father spoke. "Twelve years ago, we were told that there was little or no forensic evidence. They also never found the actual crime scene. If that was true, then there's nothing for your forensics people to work with."

"That's true, but everything will be reviewed anyway. As I told you this morning, the case has gone active again because some new information has come to light."

"The nature of which you refused to share with us, so forgive us if we don't believe you."

Aubrey stared at her mother in shock. That was a pretty outrageous statement from a woman who preached tolerance and good manners at all times. Meanwhile, her mother plowed right on ahead.

"My husband and I discussed the situation after you left this morning. Our obligation is to make the best decision for our daughter, which is to shut down this farce before it goes any farther. Her therapist is really concerned about how she continues to be fixated on that incident from twelve years ago. I spoke to him today, and he says this could exacerbate the situation."

Her mother's callous words ripped opened deep wounds that had never really healed. Her parents meant well, but

Aubrey could never find the right words to convince them that they were wrong. It was also humiliating to have them sit there and talk about her in front of Jonah Kelly as if she was incapable of making decisions for herself. This was her life they were talking about, and she was the one who was in charge of it.

When Jonah opened his mouth to respond to her mother, Aubrey shot him a hard look and shook her head. After a slight hesitation, he nodded and leaned back in his chair. She didn't doubt for one minute that he would charge right back into the fray if he thought the situation called for it.

She liked that about him.

Aubrey rose to her feet to stare down at her parents. It was tempting to scream at them, but that would only reinforce their belief that they knew what was best for her. "Mom, I'm sorry but you and Dad need to leave right now. Detective Kelly is a guest in my home, and I won't let you be rude to him. That's the first thing. Second, you've somehow forgotten that I'm an adult and have been for a long time. You may think you're protecting me, but what you're really doing is diminishing me. Third, Dr. Wilcox may be your therapist, but he definitely isn't mine. I fired him ten years ago and haven't spoken to the man since. I don't appreciate him rendering baseless opinions about me. If it continues, I will file an official complaint about his unprofessional behavior with the proper authorities."

Then she gestured toward Jonah. "As far as I'm concerned, right now Detective Kelly is the only person in this room who actually has my best interests at heart."

When her parents made no move to leave, she walked over to the door and opened it. "That wasn't a suggestion, folks. It was an order. Go home before you permanently damage our relationship, because right now it's on pretty shaky ground."

Her mother's face was ashen, and her father wasn't looking much better when he spoke for both of them. "Aubrey, we're just trying to do what's best for you."

"And failing miserably at the moment. I'm sorry if that's hurtful, but it would be nice if for once you talked with me instead of *at* me."

When they finally did as she asked, she stood by the door. As they passed by, she gave in to a strong urge to hug each of them. "I've never doubted that you love me and that you wish none of this had ever happened. So do I, but it did. I sincerely believe that the only chance I have to ever put all of this to rest is to learn the truth. I pray to our Lord every night that someday that will happen."

Her mother drew a ragged breath. "Then that's what I'll pray for, too. We'll go now."

Aubrey suspected she wasn't the only one who was seeing through a sheen of tears right now. It was tempting to slam the door shut and turn the locks. Instead, she patiently waited until they were backing out of the driveway to wave at them one last time.

Finally finding the courage to tell her parents exactly how she felt was surprisingly cathartic but also exhausting. She closed the door and leaned against it, needing its solid strength at her back while she reined in her emotions. Even with her eyes closed, she was acutely aware of the silent man watching her every move. Finally, she returned to the table.

He waited until she sat and had a sip of her tea to speak. "I'm sorry for riling them up like that."

"It's not your fault, Detective. All the blame rests squarely on the shoulders of the monster who started all of this twelve

years ago. Like I told my folks, the only way to end this
threat is to find the truth."

Despite the roller-coaster ride of emotions she'd been on
since her current companion had showed up on her doorstep yesterday, she was determined to keep moving forward. "I don't know about you, Detective Kelly, but I've
worked up quite an appetite. What do you say we order a
pizza and then figure out where we go from here?"

"I say call me Jonah, and the pizza will be my treat."

SIX

Jonah parked his car a few houses down the street from his target's home. Before making his final approach, he decided to sit back and observe for a short time. He hadn't set out to spy on Ross Easton, but just by happenstance the man was outside working out in his front yard when Jonah turned down his street.

All in all, Easton's home was picture-perfect, which was a little surprising. He'd gotten the impression from Aubrey that Ross Easton had never recovered from the loss of his fiancée in the intervening twelve years. Jonah had expected the man's home to reflect some of that dysfunction. Maybe Ross had finally moved on with his life.

Jonah hoped so.

There was only one way to find out. He drove forward to park directly in front of Easton's house. The man had just finished putting away his lawnmower. He shut the garage door and started toward his front porch, but paused when he noticed Jonah climbing out of his car.

"Can I help you?"

Jonah stopped at the curb to take out his identification before stepping on Easton's property. He held it up to show his badge and picture. "Mr. Easton, I'm Detective

Jonah Kelly. I would like to talk for a few minutes if you have time."

Easton's expression instantly morphed from friendly curiosity to disgust. "Like it's ever made any difference if I said I was busy whenever one of you shows up without even bothering to call first."

He probably wasn't wrong about that. "This shouldn't take long."

Still not looking any happier, Easton nodded. "Fine, come on in. Just know that I have to leave for work in an hour and need to get cleaned up before I go."

Jonah followed him inside and up the stairs to the main level of the house. He stopped at the top of the steps to see where his unwilling host wanted him to go. Pointing to the right, Easton said, "Might as well do this in the kitchen. I don't know about you, but I could use a drink."

He shot Jonah a hard look. "I'm talking a glass of water or iced tea, nothing alcoholic. I finally got my act together and gave that stuff up about five years back."

Interesting.

"Either would be fine."

Easton motioned toward the small kitchen table. "Make yourself comfortable. I'm going to wash my hands first, and then I'll fix the drinks."

Jonah took advantage of the delay to quietly look around the kitchen and the limited amount of the living room that he could see from where he was sitting. Nothing looked new or fancy, but it looked…cozy. That was the best description he could come up with. It was the kind of place that his mother would likely say had benefited from a woman's touch. It was difficult to decide if Easton actually had someone special in his life, though. There was only a single plate and cup in the dish drainer next to the sink, and the three pairs of shoes lined up next to the back door were all men's.

His unwilling host set two glasses of iced tea on the table and sat down. While he got settled, Jonah took a long drink. "Thanks. That hit the spot."

Easton ignored his own drink as he crossed his arms over his chest and leaned back in his chair. "Now that the pleasantries are over with, what's going on? Why are you here instead of that other guy who used to hassle me on a regular basis?"

Jonah took out his notebook and a pen. "I'm new on the case. I took over Detective Swahn's workload after he retired."

"And you decided to ruin my day by stopping by just to introduce yourself? If so, you can leave now that you've done that."

"Not exactly." He met Easton's gaze head-on. "I'm reinterviewing everyone connected to the kidnapping."

Easton reached for his iced tea and held it in a white-knuckled grip as if debating whether or not to toss it in Jonah's face. "Why can't you people simply leave the past in the past?"

There was no easy way to break the news, so Jonah launched his opening salvo. "Someone sent an anonymous note that presents a very clear and present threat to Aubrey Sims. I'm here to see if you know anything about that."

Easton's shock seemed clear-cut as he leaned forward, his elbows on the table. "Me? Why would you think that?"

"Because you used to stalk Aubrey, Mr. Easton," Jonah declared bluntly. "She has good reason to think you never forgave her for being the one who came home."

The other man's expression turned grim. "I'm not proud

of it, but she isn't wrong about that. Like a lot of fools, I tried to numb my pain with alcohol. When that didn't work, I looked for a handy target for my anger. For sure, Aubrey deserved better from me. I pretty much hit bottom, but I thank God every day that my pastor convinced me to get help. It hasn't been easy, but I haven't touched a drop of alcohol for nearly six years now."

He stared at the tabletop for several seconds as he visibly struggled to regain control. When he finally looked back up at Jonah, his eyes were full of regret. "I also haven't gone near Aubrey since I first got sober, even though I should've apologized to her. The two of us used to be friends, but I figure I burned that bridge a long time ago."

He lapsed into silence for several seconds, no doubt lost in the pain of his memories. When he finally spoke again, his words were laced with cold, hard anger. "Seriously, some joker is threatening Aubrey? Who would do that and why now?"

"I can't reveal the exact content of the note, but I assure you that the threat was very clear. As of right now, we don't know who sent the note or why they picked this particular moment in time."

"Is she okay? The poor thing has got to be scared out of her wits."

Easton's concern felt genuine, as if it really upset him that Aubrey might be in danger. Perhaps he was putting on a good act, but it was too soon to tell.

"So, Mr. Easton, when was the last time you spoke to or saw Aubrey?"

The other man stared out the window next to the table as he mulled over the question. "Look, this probably won't be the only time we'll be talking. Could you please just call me Ross? Mr. Easton feels a little too much like I'm being interrogated."

That wasn't too far off the truth. But if using his first name made the man feel more comfortable, Jonah wouldn't argue the point. "Fine, Ross it is. So, to be clear, when did you last interact with Aubrey?"

"Five years ago at least, right before I did a stint in rehab. Afterward, I started going to meetings to help stay sober. That's when I realized what I was doing wasn't right. For sure it wasn't helping either of us deal with what had happened."

"And what exactly had you been doing?"

Ross's face flushed red. "Watching over her. Following her whenever she went out. I told myself I was keeping an eye on her to make sure nothing happened to her, but that wasn't it at all. Like you said, I was stalking Aubrey, plain and simple. I count myself lucky that she didn't have me arrested for it."

He was right about that. If she'd told Jonah's predecessor what was going on, Swahn would have tossed Ross behind bars in a heartbeat. "Why were you doing that?"

"Back then, I spent a lot of time with Marta's parents. Too much time, to be honest. After a while, instead of comforting each other, we somehow revved each other up instead. It was so frustrating that the cops couldn't find the guy that did this, and we wanted...no, we *needed* someone to blame. That was especially true for Marta's mom. I don't know why, but Aubrey became the main target for Dina's anger. She was always asking why had Aubrey gotten to come home and not Marta. She went so far as to wonder what Aubrey had done to convince that kidnapper to let her go instead of Marta. That sort of thing."

Jonah fought down a surge of anger and prayed for patience. How could they not realize that Aubrey had been a victim, too? None of what happened had been her fault. But judging from the deep lines bracketing Ross's mouth and eyes, he'd suffered enough. He didn't need Jonah to read him the riot act for his past bad behavior. It was time to get back on topic.

"Do you still remember many details about what happened twelve years ago?"

Ross shivered. "Yeah, despite all the alcohol I consumed, it did nothing to dull those memories. Marta and Aubrey had a late afternoon class. They were supposed to meet up with some friends at a coffee shop afterward to review for a test they were having the next day. When neither of them showed, their friends tried calling them. After leaving several messages, they finally drove back to the college to look for Marta and Aubrey. They found Aubrey's car in the parking lot with both of its back tires slashed. The campus cops took their statements and then called the regular police. I pretty much stayed with Marta's parents around the clock for days while we waited for word."

He stopped to drink some more tea. "At first, we were all thrilled to learn Aubrey had been found and kept waiting for someone to find Marta."

His voice dropped to a rough whisper. "Twelve years later, we're still waiting."

Ross looked around the room, his eyes dull with pain. "I bought this place right after Marta and I got engaged. The only reason I could afford it was that the house was in foreclosure, and the previous owner had let it get really run-down."

He smiled just a little. "Unlike me, Marta was always

super organized, so naturally she started a notebook of everything we needed to do to fix it up. Lists of paint colors, flooring, even the style of furniture she wanted. Over the years, I've checked off nearly every item on her to-do lists. There isn't a day that goes by that I don't wish she were here to see it all. Marta would've loved seeing how close I've come to making her dreams come true."

That was probably true, but Jonah thought maybe Ross would be better off if he never looked at that notebook again. Not that he'd tell him that. He understood all too well how one tragic moment in time became the center of someone's universe. The gaping hole that Gino's death had left in Jonah's own life remained a steady ache every minute of every day. His entire life was now seen through the filter of knowing he had lived but his friend hadn't.

For now, the best Jonah could do for Ross was stay busy jotting down a few more notes to give him time to regain his composure. Finally, he picked up the interview where they'd left off. "Looking back, is there anything else you can tell me? Especially anything significant that might have happened before that evening?"

Ross closed his eyes for several seconds. "I've spent years wondering if there was something I missed…something that might've clued us in that Marta and Aubrey were in danger, but there's nothing. No near misses. No weird encounters with a stranger. No sign of anyone sneaking around or watching them. At the time, the police did their best to reconstruct Marta's movements for the week prior to her disappearance. I assume they did the same for Aubrey."

Jonah looked up from his notebook. "I know they were roommates at the college. Do you know if they had more than that one class together?"

"After all this time, I'm not sure. They were both education majors, but Aubrey was aiming for elementary school, and Marta wanted to work with older kids." Then Ross frowned. "Aubrey worked a few hours a week in the admissions office as part of her financial aid package. Marta had a part-time job in the library that she was going to quit at the end of the semester. She was leaving right after Christmas to study abroad."

"So both of them worked in positions where they might have met a wide variety of students and faculty?"

Ross gave him a curious look. "Is that important?"

"Right now I don't know what's important and what isn't. But I didn't see anything about their jobs in the file. I'll have to talk to Aubrey about it when I see her again. Is there anything else you think I should know?"

"Not that I can think of." Ross glanced at the clock on the nearby microwave. "Look, I need to get a move on if I'm going to get to work on time."

After sticking his notebook and pen back into his pocket, Jonah pulled out his business card and laid it on the table. "Call me if you think of anything. I'm sorry that I've stirred up a bunch of painful memories for you, but my priority right now has to be keeping Aubrey Sims safe."

Both men rose to their feet. To Jonah's surprise, Ross held out his hand. "Actually, it was nice being able to talk about Marta with someone who understands why I still miss her after all this time. If she'd died in an accident or something *normal*…although I'm not sure that's the right word exactly, but you get the idea…maybe I would've been able to move on. But it's the not knowing that lingers on, so there's never been any real closure for those of us who loved her. I'm guessing that's true for Aubrey, too."

He wasn't wrong about that. "Listen, I can't swear I'll succeed in finding you the answers you need, but I can promise that I'll try my best. For now, I'll let myself out so you can get ready for work."

As he walked away, Ross called after him, "Tell Aubrey I'm sorry."

"I will."

Jonah stepped out on the small porch and pulled the door closed behind him. He stopped long enough to breathe in the scent of fresh-cut grass and the scattering of flowers in bloom around the yard. It took two more breaths to clear out the miasma of misery that had permeated the very walls inside Ross's home.

Closing his eyes and lifting his face to the warmth of the sun, Jonah considered what he should do next. Finally, he silently offered up a small prayer. *Father, guide my steps so I can help You bring peace to Ross and the others connected to this case. Amen.*

He realized how good it felt to be talking to God again. And having done all he could for Ross Easton, it was time to move on to the next stop on his agenda. After that, he'd check in with Aubrey before calling it a day.

Aubrey made another round through the house to look out each and every window. It was the third time she's done so since she'd gotten home from work two hours ago. She wasn't sure exactly what she was hoping to see—or maybe not see—but she couldn't seem to resist the compulsion to keep peeking outside. It would be dark soon, so there wasn't much point in maintaining the vigil much longer.

This small house was her sanctuary, the place she always felt safe. The one thing she rarely experienced while inside its four walls was loneliness. She was comfortable in her own skin, content to spend her evening hours preparing for the next day's lessons at school or reading a good book.

That anonymous note had changed everything, leaving her wondering if she was really safe anywhere. Rather than focus on that thought, she reminded herself of all the security features she already had in place, starting with strong doors with more locks than any rational person would deem necessary. All of her windows were covered with sheets of the top-rated security film inside and out. She had also invested in a top-of-the-line alarm system that she upgraded every time a better one came on the market. None of that had come cheap, but it was all necessary as far as she was concerned.

The only question was if there was anything else she could do to ensure the person behind the note couldn't breach her home. Maybe she'd ask Jonah the next time they spoke, not that she knew when that would be. Yeah, he'd told her to call any time, but that didn't mean she should bother him unnecessarily.

Looking around for any kind of distraction, she settled on something she'd already put off longer than she should have. She settled into her favorite chair in the living room and dialed her parents' number. While she hadn't quite forgiven them for their bad behavior, at least the source of their concern was understandable. They were her parents and worrying about their only child came with the job description. The least she could do was reassure them that she was all right.

Her father picked up on the second ring. "Hi, Dad. Before I start on the stack of work I brought home from school, I thought I'd call to see what you two are up to."

"The usual. I washed the car. Your mom did the grocery shopping. We're going to watch the ball game here in a little while."

From the time Aubrey was a young girl, she and her father had spent many hours watching sports together. It was one of the few things she'd missed after she'd moved out. "I'll probably turn it on myself while I grade papers."

"Don't work too hard, sweetheart. You should be out with your friends doing something fun."

It wasn't the first time he'd made that suggestion. "It's almost the end of the school year, so I've got to get everything finished up. Two weeks from now I'll be free to kick back and relax."

Hopefully. If Jonah and his associates managed to track down the note writer by then. Until that happened, doing something fun or relaxing would was out of the question.

"Oops, kiddo, Mom is yelling that dinner's ready. I'd better go."

"Okay, Dad. Tell her hi for me. Love you both."

There was a brief silence before he spoke again. "I know it might not seem like it sometimes, but we do know you're an adult and capable of making your own decisions. We can't help but worry, though. The compulsion is an unavoidable part of the whole being-a-parent package."

She laughed, mainly because it would make him feel better. Her too, for that matter. "Enjoy the game, Dad."

As soon as she hung up, the doorbell rang. Just that quickly her good mood disappeared. Once again, she wasn't expecting anyone. Well, unless Jonah had decided to stop by without calling first. She checked the camera feed from the front door to see a young woman standing there holding a bouquet of flowers in her hand. A peek out the front window revealed a small SUV with the name of a local florist emblazoned on its exterior.

Everything seemed to be on the up-and-up, but who would be sending her flowers? There was only one way to find out. She unlocked the door and opened it just enough to be able to look out. "Hello, can I help you?"

"I have flowers for Aubrey Sims."

"I'm Aubrey."

She opened the door wider. As soon as she did, the delivery woman thrust the flower arrangement at her, leaving her no choice but to take it. "Do you know who they're from?"

"There's a card."

The woman stepped off the porch and kept going while Aubrey remained frozen in place, not sure what to do next. She was probably being foolish, but there was no way she was going to take the flowers inside her house. Not until she knew who had sent them. She loved fresh flowers as much as the next person, and the bouquet of a dozen roses in a variety of colors was gorgeous—and a seriously romantic gesture. There was a problem—she couldn't remember the last time she'd even been on a date. So there was no significant other, no boyfriend, not even a casual friend who would have forked over big bucks to buy her flowers.

That didn't mean she could just keep standing there holding the bouquet. Eventually she was going to have to take action of some kind. It was tempting to throw the flowers in her yard waste bin, but that wouldn't provide any answers. While she stood there dithering, it finally occurred to her that whoever had sent the flowers could be watching to see how she reacted. That possibility finally stirred her into action.

Rather than take the flowers inside, she gently set them on the table right there on the porch. Then, trying to act as if she was actually thrilled about the surprise bouquet, Aubrey leaned down to breathe in their perfume. Normally, she liked roses, but she found the scent of this bunch to be too strong and cloying. It was probably only her imagination working overtime, but she couldn't wait to put some distance between herself and the flowers.

After one more look around, she headed back inside the house to summon help. It was time to call Detective Kelly.

SEVEN

Jonah hung back and watched as the forensics team once again did their thing. The techs had finished taking photographs and then planned to dust everything for fingerprints. He doubted they'd learn much of anything from the flower arrangement itself, but it was important to do everything by the book. The most likely scenario was that only the employees at the florist shop had actually touched the flowers, the vase and the cardboard box that came with them.

While he dealt with the situation at Aubrey's house, Jonah had sent a patrol officer to stop by the florist shop to take preliminary statements from the owner and her employees to see what they could remember about the person who had ordered the roses. Predictably, it wasn't much. It had been a man, probably around six feet tall, with brownish hair that had been mostly covered up with a baseball cap. He'd worn sunglasses and was dressed as if on his way to play softball, right down to the batting gloves.

The bottom line was that nothing about him set off any alarms—just a regular guy sending last-minute flowers for a special occasion. He'd paid for the flowers in cash rather than with a debit or credit card. While not all that common these days, it still happened from time to time.

Even the card that had accompanied the flowers proved to be useless as evidence. The man had left the shop without filling one out. Instead, he'd called half an hour later using a burner phone to say he'd forgotten that one little detail. The florist had offered to print the card for him, something she routinely did on orders that were phoned in. The message had been short and sweet: *I'll always be grateful for the gift of sharing time with you.*

It might have all sounded innocent enough to the florist, but Jonah knew better. It was another threat aimed right at Aubrey Sims. Another message intended to terrorize her while heightening the kidnapper's own pleasure.

"Is that everything?"

The tech finished bagging the note. "As much as we can accomplish here. We'll let you know if we manage to find anything useful."

"Thanks for responding so fast."

He left them to finish up. It was time to check in with Aubrey. She'd had no interest in watching the techs deal with the flowers, which was fine with him. There was always the chance that whoever sent the bouquet was close by as the drama played out. With that in mind, Jonah had quietly monitored the small crowd of curious neighbors across the street. According to the first officer on the scene, they'd started gathering not long after he had arrived to watch over Aubrey until Jonah could get there himself. He'd been on the other side of town at his physical therapy appointment when she'd called, and he hadn't wanted her to have to wait by herself.

He snapped a few more pictures of the small crowd to show Aubrey in case she recognized anyone who shouldn't be there. After one more look up and down the street, he knocked on the front door. "Aubrey, it's Jonah. Can you let me in?"

She must have been hovering near the door, because he could hear her turning the locks almost immediately. He slipped inside as quickly as possible, figuring she wouldn't feel safe until the door was closed and secured again. Her relief was palpable as she turned the dead bolt and fastened the chain.

He held out his phone. "I'd like you to look at these pictures I took of the people watching from across the street. They're most likely your neighbors, but I'd like to verify that if at all possible."

She glanced at the phone and then shook her head. "I will in a minute. I just made a fresh pot of tea and thought you might like some. I also thawed some banana bread I had in the freezer."

While he'd prefer to get right down to business, it was obvious that she needed the little bit of normalcy playing hostess would give her before she could deal with the current situation. "Tea actually sounds good. I usually take it with two sugars, no milk."

"Have a seat, and I'll be right back."

Half of the dining room table was covered in rows of folders made out of large sheets of brightly colored construction paper. There was a single name written at the top of each one, no doubt the members of her class. He had to admire Aubrey's determination to keep up with the needs of her students despite what was going on in her own life.

Which meant she wasn't going to appreciate what he was about to suggest. Whoever was behind the note and the flowers was definitely amping up his game. After twelve years of total silence, all of a sudden the kidnapper had reached out to Aubrey twice in less than a week. That didn't bode well for the coming days when they currently had no idea who the guy was, where he was located, or what his personal timeline looked like. To make matters worse, the man also knew both where Aubrey received her mail and her actual street address.

All of that made it much more likely that Aubrey had been right about someone following her recently. Jonah didn't know about her, but he knew he'd sleep better at night knowing that she was tucked away somewhere safe and sound.

As promised, she returned with their refreshments. After setting the tray down, she gathered up the files into a neat pile and set them out of the way on the far corner of the table. "Pardon the mess. I always send a folder of my students' best work home with them on the last day of school. They get to decorate the folders as an art project."

"I'm sure their parents love that."

At least his own parents had liked stuff like that. Meanwhile, Aubrey set his tea in front of him along with a plate with two thick slices of banana bread. "I didn't know if you liked the bread with anything on it, but I brought both butter and cream cheese."

"Plain would have been fine, but cream cheese sounds good."

As he spread a thick layer on the bread, Aubrey did the same with the butter. When she set her knife down, she gave him a tentative look. "Are they gone?"

It wasn't clear if she was talking about the forensics team or the flowers themselves. He decided to cover all the bases. "The techs were packing up to leave when I knocked on your door. They took everything with them—the flowers, the vase, the packing materials and the card."

Her relief was obvious. She took a small bite of the banana bread and then washed it down with a sip of tea. After setting her mug back down on the table, she visibly braced herself and asked, "Were you able to learn anything from the card?"

"Unfortunately, no. The guy didn't write it himself, so we can't compare the handwriting to the previous note. He paid cash, gave them your address and then left. The florist printed the note for him and stuck it in the envelope."

"What was the message?"

Jonah really didn't want to tell her. It wasn't just the message; it was the type of card he'd requested. "Something about being grateful for your time together."

Aubrey flinched as if the words actually caused her physical pain. He figured that was likely true. She picked up her mug and wrapped both hands around it, maybe needing that touch of warmth. A second later, she made eye contact with him and set the mug back down hard enough to splash some over the rim. After shaking the hot tea off her skin, she frowned at him. "There's more, isn't there? About the card, I mean. Something worse."

It was tempting to lie, but he needed her to trust him. "Yeah. It was a sympathy card, the kind that normally accompanies flowers sent to a funeral home."

Jonah gave her time to absorb that little bombshell and regroup before they continued. To his surprise, she simply nodded and then pointed toward his phone, which he'd laid on the table. "You wanted me to look at some pictures?"

He brought up the first one and handed her the phone. "I took them at different times, trying to capture the faces of everyone who stopped to watch. Even if you don't know them by name, it will help me narrow down anyone we need to check into."

She quickly flipped through the pictures one after the other without saying anything, and then went back to the first one. After setting the phone on the table, she scooted her chair a little closer to his so they could both see the screen. "All three people in this first one live on this block. The additional guy in the second one lives on the next street over. He walks his dog down our block almost every day about this time."

"That's helpful to know."

She was probably relieved to recognize everyone he'd photographed. Personally, he was disappointed but not surprised. It was too much to hope that there would have been a guy in a ball cap and gloves carrying a sign saying he'd sent the flowers. Time to move on.

After returning his phone to his jacket pocket, he brought up the next subject on his list. "So, I met with Ross Easton at his house."

That actually caused Aubrey to perk up a bit. "How is he?"

Leave it to her to care more about how her former stalker was doing than if he was any kind of threat to her. "From what I could tell, he's doing okay. More or less, anyway. I'm no psychologist, but I think that it means something that he's taking good care of his house and yard. He's holding down a job, too. I checked with his boss earlier today, and he says Ross is a hard worker and reliable."

"That's good news. He bought that house for him and Marta to live in after they got married. I kind of wondered if he'd sold it. Too many memories, you know."

Jonah decided not to tell her about Marta's notebook and how Ross had spent years creating the home she had wanted but that they would never share. Instead, he focused on the good news, such as it was. "He said his pastor helped him get into a rehab program five or six years ago. He claims he hasn't had a drink since."

He paused to take a sip of his tea. "He also said that once he got sober, he'd considered reaching out to apologize to you. In the end, he figured by that point you wouldn't want to hear from him. Regardless, he was upset that someone was threatening you now and was adamant it wasn't him."

"And you believed him?"

Jonah had given that particular question a lot of serious thought after leaving Ross's house. "Yeah, I did. He wasn't happy when I first showed up, but he definitely switched gears once I explained someone had threatened you. He didn't deny what happened before, but immediately swore he wasn't involved this time. I believe he was genuinely upset by what's been going on."

Aubrey sat in silence as she drank more of her tea and nibbled on a small bite of banana bread. Finally, she said, "If you talk to Ross again, please tell him that his apology is accepted. I guess we all handle grief in different ways. He had his life with Marta planned out. They were so happy together, and someone stole that away from him. It must have felt as if he'd lost half of himself."

Her description of what Ross had experienced hit a little too close to home for Jonah. Yeah, he'd lost his partner, but Gino's family had lost so much more—father, husband, son. All those relationships destroyed because one man got scared and decided to start shooting. Jonah was long overdue to stop by and check on Gino's wife and kids.

They always seemed happy to see him, but he often wondered how long that would last. He wanted them to know that he'd come running whenever they needed him, but he feared that eventually he would become a painful reminder of what all they'd lost.

An unexpected movement near his face startled him, causing him to jerk his head back and almost go diving for cover. A second later, he realized that it was Aubrey waving her hand in front of his eyes as she tried to get his attention. He snapped, "What?"

Before she could explain, he immediately apologized. "Sorry, I didn't mean to snarl. I got lost in thought there for a second, and you surprised me."

Her expression turned sympathetic as she sat back in her chair and out of his reach. "It was more than a second, Jonah. You stopped talking and then just sat there staring off into space. I don't know where you went in your head, but I'm guessing it wasn't a good place."

Aubrey had enough problems on her plate without having to hear about his. "I'm okay. It was nothing."

Her skepticism was clear as she scoffed, "You might tell yourself that, but I don't believe it for a second. It wasn't nothing, Jonah. I've seen that same look in my own eyes too many times to believe that. What's going on?"

He found it interesting how she could look fragile one second and so fierce the next. He'd first seen it happen when she defended him against her parents. He found her inner core of strength fascinating. Meanwhile, she arched an eyebrow, still waiting for him to explain. He only realized that he was rubbing his knee when she gave it a pointed look. "Does it have something to do with how you hurt your leg?"

Despite his determination to keep his history private, the words slipped out. "I took a bullet in my knee when a case went sideways."

No sooner did he speak than he somehow found himself holding Aubrey's hand. Not at all sure how that had happened, he forced himself to release it and tried to rebuild the emotional barrier he lived behind these days. She didn't try to stop him, but that didn't mean she was letting the matter drop. "I think I heard about that on the news."

Then she gasped. "You weren't the only one who was shot that night, were you?"

"No, I wasn't. My partner was killed." He stared down at the half-eaten banana bread on his plate as if it were the most fascinating thing he'd ever seen. "Gino left behind a wife and kids. I can't help but keep wondering why him and not me. They needed him, while I didn't have anyone waiting at home for me."

"You can't think that way, Jonah. You didn't pull the trigger. That's all on the other guy. You know your friend wouldn't have blamed you. He knew the dangers that come along with being a cop, but he chose to serve anyway. You should honor his service and his memory, but don't let it keep you from getting on with your own life."

That was rich coming from her. He knew she meant well, but did she really think she had been successful at that? Yeah, she held down a steady job. She took good care of her house, but so did her old friend Ross. All of that was superficial, keeping up appearances in an effort to fool the world—and themselves—that everything was okay. But in so many ways, the two of them had stopped living life to the fullest twelve years ago. A glance at Aubrey's front door was proof of that. How many people had a security chain, a dead bolt, and two other heavy-duty locks on their front door?

When she noticed where he was looking, she literally shrank in on herself. Her shoulders slumped and her arms wrapped around her waist as if to ease her pain. "I guess I don't have any room to talk. In fact, forget I said anything at all. Rather than offering advice, I should stick to asking if you'd like some ibuprofen."

Then she picked up her plate and mug and disappeared into the kitchen.

EIGHT

Aubrey dumped the rest of her tea down the drain and stuck the mug in the dishwasher. She followed it with her plate after brushing the last crumbs of her banana bread into the trash. With that done, she looked around for something else to give her shaky hands something productive to do. She settled for getting the ibuprofen out of the cabinet and filling a juice glass with water just as Jonah stepped into the small confines of the kitchen.

"I'm sorry, Aubrey."

"For what exactly, Detective Kelly? Like I said, I'm the last one who should try telling someone how to deal with tragedy."

She pointed toward the glass of water and the pills on the counter. "Help yourself, and then you should leave. I still have a lot of work to do tonight. Thank you for coming when I called."

"It's my job."

Why didn't that make her feel better about the whole situation? "I'm guessing it's well past your normal quitting time. You can see yourself out."

Meanwhile, Jonah took two ibuprofen and washed them down with the water. After setting the empty glass down, he paused to study her, his eyebrows riding low over his eyes. "Look, Aubrey, I didn't mean—"

She cut him off. "It's been a long day for both of us, so just go. I'll call you if anything else comes up that I think you need to know about."

"There is one more thing we need to talk about before I go."

What now? Ordering him to leave again wasn't going to work, not until he had his say. She leaned against the kitchen counter and crossed her arms over her chest. "I'm listening."

"I think we should look into moving you someplace safer. You should also take a leave of absence from your job."

That so wasn't happening. She needed the routine of work, and this house was her sanctuary, the one place where she could breathe. She couldn't imagine staying anywhere else, so she focused on his second suggestion. "My students depend on me. You can't really think I would abandon them so close to the end of the year."

Although she hadn't phrased it as a question, he treated it as one. "Yes, that's exactly what I mean. You're in danger, Aubrey. I know it, and you do, too. We have no idea who is after you, but it's only a matter of time before he makes his next move. Right now, he appears to be having fun toying with you, but he's also busying finalizing his plans. If this is really the same guy, don't forget how he managed to snatch you and Marta from a busy college campus with no one being the wiser. How hard do you think it will be for him to do something similar this time? Especially if you insist on hiding your head in the sand."

It might be a losing battle, but she wasn't going to surrender easily. "But I have responsibilities. I'll stick close to home for now. You know, have my groceries delivered and stuff like that. I'll only drive from here to school and back."

Jonah took a half step closer to her. "I can't force you to do anything, Ms. Sims. You might not care about your own safety, but think about the effect of having you disappear again will have on your mom and dad. They might be helicopter parents, but what they really are is terrified that what happened to Marta will happen to you."

For the space of a heartbeat, his expression softened. "For the record, so am I."

Without giving her a chance to respond to that shocking statement, he walked away. "Don't forget to lock the door after I go."

Yeah, like that would ever happen. She trailed after him, glad he was leaving even if a part of her wished he wouldn't. After stepping out onto the porch, Jonah started to walk away but turned back one last time. "Call me if anything happens, no matter how small, or even if you simply need to talk."

Somehow, that sounded more like an apology than him issuing another order.

"I will. Thank you for coming today. I know you must have other cases that require your attention, and I appreciate how much time you've spent working on mine."

Not wanting to hear another reminder that it was his job, she quietly closed the door and starting turning the locks.

By the time Aubrey got to work the next morning, her nerves were stretched to the breaking point. The fact that she'd barely been able to sleep at all was beside the point. Over the past twelve years, she'd developed a few techniques for dealing with sleeplessness: gulping down some warm milk, listening to soothing music, drinking chamomile tea, getting up and going through her bedtime routine all over again. All of those things usually worked with some degree of success, but not last night.

On the way to school, she had decided she deserved a little treat and made a quick stop at the drive-through of her favorite coffee shop to buy a latte and a peach scone. One sip of the coffee brightened her mood considerably, even if her conscience twinged a little over taking the short detour. After all, she'd promised Jonah that she would drive straight to and from school without stopping. At least there hadn't been anyone in line ahead of her, so the delay was minimal. She pulled back out into traffic and drove the last distance to the school.

When she reached the parking lot, Jonah's car was parked in the front row. What was he doing there? She pulled into the spot next to his and got out. He did the same.

She gathered up everything she needed to take inside with her. It took some juggling on her part to manage her canvas tote, her purse, the latte and the bag containing her scone. Once she had everything situated, she walked around to the back of her car where Jonah stood. As he waited, he quietly scanned the surrounding area. Was he expecting trouble? She did a quick survey herself and then frowned at him. "Did we have an appointment that I forgot about?"

"I wanted to make sure you got to work all right."

She stated the obvious. "Obviously I did."

He finally looked down at her. "So it would appear. Do you need help schlepping all of that stuff inside?"

Ever the gentleman. "No, I do this all the time. Thanks for checking on me."

"Anything to report?"

"I didn't sleep all that well, but that happens from time to time." Noting the dark circles under Jonah's eyes, she added, "I suppose you have your own experience with nights like that."

He shrugged. "Comes with the job. I'll walk you to the door."

Stubborn man. "I can get there on my own."

His mouth twitched in a hint of a grin. "I know that. It's the fact that your hands are full that makes me question your ability to actually open the door."

Okay, he wasn't exactly wrong about that. "Fine, it's this way."

"I'd also like to get a look at your classroom since I'm already here. Stuff like where it's located and the layout of it. It won't take long."

So he wasn't just being polite or helpful. She surrendered her keys to her classroom. "Fine, but you'll have to stop in the office to sign in. They keep track of outsiders coming in and out of the building."

"I'd rather not tell them I'm a cop. Is it okay if I tell them I'm just a friend?"

No doubt she'd get grilled by her coworkers after he left about this unexpected man in her life, but there wasn't much she could do about that. "It's fine."

Viola, the school secretary, had Jonah sign his name on the clipboard she kept on the counter for visitors to sign on their way in and out of the building and then gave him a temporary badge. When he turned his back to her, she waggled her eyebrows and gave Aubrey a thumbs-up. Over the years they'd worked together at the school, Viola had often questioned why an attractive young woman like Aubrey didn't have a man in her life. No doubt she'd corner her at the first opportunity to complain about her keeping secrets. Great. Either Aubrey would have to lie to her friend, or she'd have to tell her the truth and have another person worry about every move she made. The trouble with that was that Aubrey had never told anyone she worked with about the kidnapping.

"My classroom is this way."

The two of them drew a lot of attention as they made their way down the hallway. Several of her friends had looked a bit wide-eyed as they passed by, causing to Jonah lean in closer to ask, "Do you always create such a stir like this?"

"It's not me they're curious about, it's you. They're not used to seeing me with a man, especially a handsome one."

Her blunt assessment of his appearance had Jonah looking a bit uncomfortable, which she found amusing. The man had to own a mirror and know what he looked like. At the moment, he was sharply dressed in a dark navy suit with a white shirt and red tie. The color combination played nicely with his wavy blond hair and bright blue eyes. His limp was a little more pronounced than usual, but it did nothing to make him less attractive.

"It's this next room."

When he pulled her keys out of his suit pocket, she pointed out the right key for him. "The lock is a bit temperamental. You might have to wiggle the key a little to get it to turn."

She hustled into the room as soon as he opened the door and headed for her desk to unload everything. "If I'd known you were going to be here, I would have bought you a coffee, too."

He eyed the cup in her hand. "I thought you were going to drive to and from work without stopping."

"I never got out of the car, and there was no line. Otherwise, I wouldn't have stopped."

He gave the barest of nods as he wandered through the classroom, pausing to stare out the window toward the playground. "You should lower the blinds and close them. Anyone could be out there watching you."

She joined him by the window. "This place feels like a cave when the blinds are closed."

Jonah gave her a sideways glance, his expression all serious cop. "Better a cave than dead."

"He wouldn't shoot me." That much she was sure of.

"I never said he'd be aiming at you. In the ensuing chaos, he might even have a fair chance to grab you before anyone noticed."

His words, delivered in a chilling monotone, brought her up short. Was she endangering her students and colleagues just by showing up at work? "Do you really think that's true?"

"I don't think we can afford to discount anything at this point. It's not as if we have any clue how this guy operates these days. Kidnapping you and Marta on a busy college campus shows that he's willing to take chances."

She wasn't sure if it was her coffee or his words that left such a bitter taste in her mouth. "You said you were searching the records for similar cases. Did you find any?"

"Not so far, but that doesn't necessarily mean anything. Chances are that his pattern was still evolving back then, and he's had twelve years to hone his skills."

While she digested that grim statement, Jonah walked toward the door in the corner that opened directly onto the playground. She remained where she was while he stepped outside to study the school grounds.

By the time he returned, she had surrendered to the inevitable. "I'll talk to my principal today about taking a leave of absence for the rest of the year. It's too late for me to call for a substitute today, and I'll need a day to organize everything for whoever they hire to replace me."

"I know this is hard for you, Aubrey, but it's the smart thing to do. I'd suggest that you tell him that it's a medical or family emergency."

"I'm not disagreeing, but why do you think I should lie to my boss?"

He looked slightly more sympathetic now that she'd given in to his suggestion. "Because you never know who people talk to outside of work. The fewer people who know the truth of what is going on, the safer you'll be."

It must be hard to be so distrustful of everyone, but she supposed he'd learned that lesson the hard way. During the night when she couldn't sleep, she'd given in to the urge to learn more about when Jonah had gotten shot. Apparently, he and his partner had been meeting with an informant in regard to a case. Before that night, they'd had a long-term relationship with the guy and no reason to think he posed any threat to them. As it turned out, he'd let slip the upcoming meeting to the wrong person, an ex-con who had a real grudge against Gino from a prior case. He'd threatened the informer's wife and kids unless he turned on the two cops. The rest was history.

Jonah's phone buzzed. "I've got to take this."

Probably needing a little privacy, he stepped back outside onto the playground. Whatever the call was about had him pacing up and down in front of her windows, repeatedly clenching his free hand in a fist. It was none of her business, but she couldn't help but wonder if it was about her. When he glanced in the window and then deliberately turned his back again, she figured she had her answer.

He'd either tell her or else he wouldn't. Until Jonah made up his mind, she kept herself busy lowering the blinds and then closing them. When he came back inside, he looked at them and gave her a nod of approval. "You're right about the whole cave thing, but safety precautions outweigh classroom aesthetics."

Okay, that was funny.

"I'm going to head out. Thanks for making the right decision."

She drew a ragged breath and looked around the classroom, one of the two places that she'd felt safe. "I really hate that this is happening. I'm so tired of being afraid all of the time."

Jonah had been heading for the door, but he did an about-face and came right back to her. Instead of offering her words of comfort or issuing another lecture on how to stay safe, he enfolded her in his arms and held her close. "We'll get through this, Aubrey. I'll do whatever it takes to prevent this guy from getting his hands on you."

She believed him, but it was his warmth and strength that helped the most. It had been so very long since she'd experienced the simple comfort of another person's touch. Yeah, her parents hugged her, but it wasn't the same. Jonah was a warrior, a hero, the kind of man who would stand between her and the world if that was what it took to keep her safe. Not that she would want him to sacrifice himself like that, but it gladdened her heart to know that he actually cared that much.

He released his hold on her when she gently pushed against his chest. Stepping back, he mumbled, "That was probably unprofessional of me."

"I won't tell if you don't."

She wasn't sure which of them was more flustered about what had just happened. Judging by the way he was looking everywhere but at her and the way her pulse was racing, it was pretty much a tie. "You'd better go. You have better things to do than babysit me. I'll let you know what happens about my request to take a leave of absence. I will have to work tomorrow, but that should give them enough time to get someone in place."

He wasn't happy about the delay, but at least he didn't argue.

"Call me when you're ready to head home after school. If I can't be here to follow you back to the house, I'll ask one of the patrol cars to escort you."

She didn't have it in her to protest. "Okay. I usually get off at four o'clock, but I will probably need to stay late to get things organized."

"See you then." He hesitated. "That call was from my captain. Earlier this morning, I reached out to Mr. and Mrs. Pyne to tell them I would be stopping by to talk to them today. It won't come as a surprise that they didn't want me to come anywhere near them. I explained that they could either talk to me in the comfort of their own home, or else I would have them brought into police headquarters."

Aubrey could just imagine how well that went over with the couple, but there wasn't anything she could do about it. She'd already tried without success to convince Jonah to leave Marta's parents out of this mess. There was no reason to think she'd meet with any more success now. "What did your captain have to say about it?"

"Captain Martine backed my play, but he wanted to remind me to go easy on them if at all possible. I'm well aware that they're victims, too, and I feel bad that this will stir up a lot of bad memories for them. Having said that, I have to do my job. No one else is going to die on my watch."

Then he was gone.

NINE

Jonah pulled out of the school parking lot and turned right, the opposite direction from where he needed to go. His next stop was to meet with Mr. and Mrs. Pyne, but he had to get his head back on straight before he faced off with them. Right now, his thoughts were spiraling out of control, all of them circling around the stubborn woman he'd just left. That hug had been a huge mistake. As he'd told her, it had been unprofessional. But beyond that, it could compromise their working relationship.

Even before the shooting, Jonah had known better than to get attached to the civilians he dealt with in the course of his job. Emotions only confused things, and all too often lives depended on clear thinking. But somehow, the rules didn't seem to apply when it came to Aubrey Sims. Maybe it was the aura of solitude that surrounded her. He wasn't sure he'd ever known anyone who seemed more alone than she did.

It wasn't that she didn't have any friends. That much was clear from the way her coworkers responded to her back at the school. She must also have friends at church. Still, he wondered how well any of those people actually knew her. How much of her past had she shared with them? After all, the abduction had taken place twelve years ago while she was away at college. Old friends and relatives would know for sure, but somehow he couldn't picture her bringing up what had happened to her in the course of casual conversation. She probably worried it would change how people saw her—as a victim rather than a survivor.

It would make sense that her pastor perhaps knew at least the bare bones of her kidnapping. With luck, he'd actually been around when it all went down. If so, Jonah hoped the man had really been there for Aubrey. It helped a person to deal with the lingering effects of trauma to have someone you felt safe enough with to express your grief, your pain and, most of all, your anger. That last one was the biggie.

Jonah had been blessed to have two people who'd stepped up to help him. One was the psychologist the police department had recommended. It hadn't taken Jonah long to realize that Dr. Borrelli had plenty of experience helping officers cope with all the ugliness their jobs threw at them on a daily basis. It hadn't taken him long to convince Jonah that whatever he was feeling was okay.

The other person Jonah had turned to was Reverend Kim Waring, the assistant pastor at his church. She'd listened to everything he'd said without judgment and with endless patience when he couldn't find the words. Kim had also prayed with and for Jonah, and even understood why his friend's death had shaken his faith. Her calm demeanor had helped soothe his anger, and her advice about moving forward had gone a long way toward helping him pick up the pieces of his life.

He was pretty sure that Aubrey hadn't been that lucky. Yes, her parents had tried their best to shield her from the aftermath of the kidnapping. However, their forget-it-and-move-on philosophy, even if well-intentioned, hadn't been the right choice for Aubrey. All it did was force her to hide her true feelings from them. Knowing she'd never told her parents that she'd hired private investigators to look into her case was proof of that.

As he waited for a stoplight to turn green, he slammed his fist on the steering wheel, frustrated on so many levels. All of this was getting him nowhere. Aubrey's relationship with her parents was none of his business as long as it didn't impede his investigation. He'd do them both more good by reestablishing some professional distance between them for both their sakes. That meant getting on with his agenda for the day. He'd start by talking to the Pynes. Afterward, he was supposed to meet with his captain to give him an update on Aubrey's situation as well as a couple of other cases.

He'd also planned to call George Swahn and ask if he could meet Jonah for breakfast near the precinct in the morning. He wanted to pick George's brain to see if the man had anything in his private notes that might help Jonah get a better handle on Aubrey's case. He hoped so, because right now Jonah was chasing shadows.

His itinerary for the day set, he turned back toward the part of town where the Pynes lived.

Considering the length of time it took someone to answer when Jonah rang the doorbell, he had to wonder if the Pynes had decided to ignore him or, more likely, left home in order to avoid him altogether. He was about to ring the bell a second time when he finally heard the scuffle of footsteps inside the house. He stepped back and waited impatiently for the door to open.

The man who peeked out at him appeared to be far older than Aubrey's father. It was hard to tell if that was actually true or if it was the loss of his daughter that had left Riley Pyne stooped and fragile-looking. He squinted at Jonah as if he wasn't accustomed to bright sunshine. "What do you want?"

Jonah flashed his ID. "I'm Detective Kelly, Mr. Pyne. We spoke on the phone."

"And I told you we didn't want to talk to you."

Seriously? Were they still going to play this game? He'd promised his captain that he'd tread softly with these folks, but his patience would only last so long. "Yes, sir, I know you did. However, I wouldn't be here if it wasn't important. If you'll give me a little time to explain the situation and answer a few questions, I will do my best to not bother you again. I can't promise that the current situation won't require me to reach out again, but please understand that I won't unless I have no other options."

"Let him in, Riley."

Jonah wasn't the only one who hadn't noticed Dina Pyne had joined her husband. She was still talking. "Let's get this over with."

Turning her attention to Jonah, she studied him with angry eyes. "Nothing you have to say today will bring our daughter home after all this time. I want to hear why you want to torment us like this."

Her husband huffed a disgusted sigh, but then he stepped aside and opened the door wide enough to allow Jonah to come inside. As soon as he crossed the threshold, he wanted to go into full retreat. The inside of the house was dank and dark. It provided an interesting contrast to Ross Easton's house. He kept his polished and shiny, partly in memorial for the woman he'd loved, and maybe because on some level he hung on to some small bit of hope that life was still worth living without her in it.

Marta's parents' home reeked of their despair. After years of waiting and wondering, they'd given up on ever finding out what had become of her. The two of them existed, going through the motions only because they didn't know what else to do. Jonah prayed that somehow he could find a way to give them closure and maybe a little peace.

Before that could happen, he had to solve this threat to Aubrey.

The older couple shuffled their way down the narrow hallway to the family room. They settled into matching recliners, which left the couch for him.

After he was seated, he started in. "Let me give you a brief overview of what has been happening, which will explain why I felt it was necessary that we speak."

He stuck to the highlights to keep thing moving along at a quick pace. He ended with the delivery of the flowers, but didn't mention that Aubrey was taking a leave of absence. "And that's pretty much all of it in a nutshell. As I explained on the phone, I only recently took over the case after the previous detective retired. I'm speaking with everyone I can who was connected to the case twelve years ago."

Mr. Pyne looked slightly less angry than when Jonah first arrived. "So you think it's the same guy who took our daughter and Aubrey back then."

"Yeah, but we don't know that for sure." He leaned forward, resting his elbows on his knees. "Having said that, it seems to be highly likely. The note definitely hinted at insider knowledge."

"How is Aubrey dealing with all of this?"

Jonah was a little surprised by the concern in Mrs. Pyne's voice. "As well as can be expected. She's understandably scared."

"Poor girl. None of this has been easy for her." Mrs. Pyne's eyes glittered with a sheen of tears. "To my everlasting shame, my actions only made it worse for her. Even back then, my head knew none of it was Aubrey's fault, but my heart was broken. All that anger had to go somewhere, and I aimed it right at her."

Platitudes wouldn't change a thing, but asking for their help might. "Can you think back to right before the kidnapping took place and tell me everything you remember about that time in your daughter's life?"

Unfortunately, there wasn't much new in what they shared. Well, except one thing. Ross had indicated Marta was still working at the school library when she was kidnapped. According to her parents, Marta had already quit. She'd never actually told them much about what had happened, but they thought maybe she'd had a problem with another student. She'd assured them it was no big deal, and she would've had to quit soon anyway.

At least it was something to talk to Aubrey about. Detective Swahn, too, for that matter. Jonah stuck his pen and notebook back into his pocket and stood up. He set one of his business cards on the coffee table. "Here's my number if you think of anything else. Thank you again for talking to me today. I know this wasn't easy for you."

With some effort, Mr. Pyne pushed himself up out of his chair. "I can't say I'm happy about having all of this brought up again, Detective, but we understand why you had to do it."

He started back down the hall to open the door. As Jonah walked out, Mr. Pyne whispered, "It was nice to talk about our daughter with someone. Most folks are afraid to mention her name for fear of upsetting us, but it hurts worse when they act like she never existed at all."

There wasn't much Jonah could say to that. "I should be going."

Mr. Pyne followed him out onto the porch. "At this late date, it won't change a thing, but I sure hope you can bring the man who stole my Marta to justice."

"Me, too, Mr. Pyne. Me, too."

Aubrey was exhausted. She'd managed to meet with her principal during her lunch break. He hadn't exactly been angry that she had to leave for the rest of the year, but he wasn't happy about it either. She'd given him a list of substitutes she liked and agreed to work one more day to give him a chance to make the necessary arrangements.

A school was a small world, and it didn't take long for the news to spread about it being Aubrey's last day tomorrow. Understandably, it had generated a lot of questions. She'd fielded them as best she could while trying to avoid giving too many specifics about the nature of the emergency. She regretted that she and Jonah hadn't come up with a plausible explanation before he'd left that morning. Desperate to offer up something believable, she'd said that it was a personal family matter and left it at that.

Keeping secrets from her friends didn't sit well with her, but it was better than having to explain what was really going on. She could only imagine how they would all freak out if she were to confess a threat from her past had resurfaced, a true life-and-death situation. There was never an easy way to admit she'd been the victim of a kidnapping. The few times the subject had come up in conversation, the response from the other person had been difficult to predict. Sympathy and horror were the most common reactions, but occasionally the other person wanted to know all of the dark and twisted details of Aubrey's experience. Those were the worst times.

Eventually, she was going to have to tell her friends the truth, but that was a problem for another day. Right now, she needed to make sure she had everything she needed to take home with her. She'd already texted Jonah that she was ready to leave. He'd answered that he was on his way. After taking one last glance around the room, she picked up her stuff and left, stopping only to lock the classroom door behind her.

The hall outside was deserted. No surprise there since it was after six o'clock. Normally the only people likely to be in the building at that hour were the evening janitor and maybe the principal. Lyle often worked late, especially if there was a meeting at the district office or some event going on at the school during the evening.

She started down the hall, hating the way her footsteps rang out in the otherwise silent building. Jonah had asked if she wanted to wait for him to come to her classroom, but she'd told him that wouldn't work since the building would be locked by that point. Now she wished she'd told him to circle around the building to the door that opened to the playground. Too late now.

As she neared the school office, she spotted the janitor stepping out of a classroom a few doors down. Ruben waved at her and called, "Do you need help carrying stuff out to your car?"

"No, I've got it all."

He set down the bag of trash he was carrying and started toward her. "What's this I hear about tomorrow being your last day? You'll be back next year, won't you?"

"For sure. It's just a personal problem I have to take care of."

His smile was sympathetic. "I'm sorry to hear that, and I hope it's nothing serious."

There wasn't much she could say to that, so she changed the subject. "I should warn you that I cleaned out a bunch of stuff today, so the trash cans in my room are overflowing. I wanted to make sure everything is in good order when my substitute starts."

He waved off her concern. "Don't worry. I'll take care of it."

"Thanks, Ruben."

It was time to get going. It wouldn't be fair to keep Jonah waiting out in the parking lot any longer than necessary. Ruben had started down the hall but circled back in her direction. "I just realized how late it is. If you don't feel comfortable heading out to an empty parking lot alone, I'll walk you out to your car."

Rubin was known to offer to escort any of the women who stayed later than usual at the school. Normally she would've told him that wasn't necessary, especially when it was still light outside. Under the circumstances, though, maybe it wouldn't be a bad idea. "There's no need for you to walk me all the way out, but you can keep an eye on me from the door if you want."

He hesitated. "If you're sure."

"It will be fine. I have a friend coming to meet me. He's on his way and should be here any minute."

Ruben was near retirement age and had grandkids. She knew that because he took such delight in sharing pictures of his family members every chance he got. He also tended to treat all of the school staff, regardless of age or gender, as if they were extensions of his family. "I hope your young man is treating you right."

She went with the safest answer she could think of. "So far, so good."

Then she ducked out of the door to avoid any further discussion on the subject. There was still no sign of Jonah, but surely he'd be there any second. As she got closer to her car, she noticed there was something odd about the way it looked, as if it was listing to one side. Her steps slowed as she tried to make sense of what she was seeing, which didn't take long. Suddenly, she was flashing back to twelve years as she and Marta had walked out to her car in the college parking lot to find her tires had been slashed. This time, someone had driven a spike into her rear tire.

Her blood ran cold—her stalker had struck again.

TEN

Aubrey remained frozen in place, breathing hard and looking around in panic. Was the culprit still nearby, waiting to grab her again? Unlike the college parking lot, there were no nearby bushes or any other hiding spot close by. That didn't mean she was safe. The sound of an approaching car had her backing up several steps, ready to break and run back toward the school.

At the last second, she realized it was her boss's SUV. That was a relief. The sound of footsteps coming from behind had her glancing back over her shoulder. Just as she'd hoped, it was Ruben heading her way.

"Is something wrong, Ms. Aubrey?"

"Unfortunately, yes. Someone vandalized my tire." She pointed toward her car. "They rammed some kind of spike in it."

His usual genial expression turned grim. "Who would do something awful like that? And right out here in the open, too?"

"No idea."

Okay, that was a lie. Sort of. It was true that she didn't know the perpetrator's name or even what he looked like. By that point, Principal Peale was out of his vehicle. He stopped to study her car before joining her and Ruben on the sidewalk. "Aubrey, are you okay? Did either of you see anything?"

Ruben shook his head. "I've been working in the rooms that face the back of the building."

Aubrey did her best to sound calm. "I'm fine, but I didn't see anything, either. For sure, there was no one around when I came out of the building."

Lyle stood with his hands on his hips as he studied their surroundings. He looked pretty disgusted by the whole affair. "I can't believe someone would do something like this. We should probably call the police."

He pulled out his phone just as another car turned into the lot. Aubrey breathed a sigh of relief when she saw it was Jonah. He pulled into the spot next to hers and hustled over to where she was standing. "Aubrey, what's happened?"

Gesturing to her companions, she said, "My friend Ruben was watching from the front door to make sure that I made it to my car okay. When I saw the condition of my tire, I was going to go back inside the building to wait for you, but that's when my boss arrived. Lyle Peale is our principal, and Ruben Jacobs is the evening custodian here at the school."

The two men gave her identical expectant looks, obviously waiting for her to continue the introductions. "And this is my friend Detective Jonah Kelly."

Jonah nodded at her coworkers in turn. "Gentlemen."

None of them seemed inclined to shake hands. She wasn't sure what to make of that, considering both her boss and Ruben were normally friendly and outgoing. That said, she had to admit this didn't exactly feel like a social situation. Jonah walked around to the driver's side of her car and squatted down to study the damage. After snapping a couple of quick pictures, he rejoined her on the side-walk. "Are you okay?"

Not really, but she figured she could hold it together until she got home. "Yeah, I was startled when I first saw the damage. Now, I'm more mad than anything."

That made him smile. "I can understand why. I'll call it in for you. After the patrol officer takes your statement, I'll change your tire."

Jonah kept his eyes on her as he made the call. As soon as he hung up, he peeled off his suit coat and draped it across Aubrey's shoulders. It was a warm evening, but she was chilled to the bone. "Thanks."

"No problem. The patrol officer should be here any minute."

Ruben didn't look convinced. "I called the police when somebody broke a window in one of the classrooms a couple of months back. It took them two hours to get here."

He'd no sooner said that than a police car turned into the parking lot, its lights flashing. Jonah looked down at Aubrey. "I'll be right back."

He walked down to meet the police officer and talked to her in a low voice. Then he led her around to look at the damage to Aubrey's car before coming back to where Aubrey waited with Ruben and Principal Peale.

The officer had a clipboard with a form on it, her pen poised to take notes. "Hi, I'm Officer Goff."

Jonah introduced Aubrey. "This is Ms. Sims. She worked later than usual and came out to find that someone had driven a spike into her tire."

The officer gave Aubrey a curious look. "I'm sorry that happened. Did you happen to see anything?"

Aubrey shook her head. "Like Detective Kelly said, I

worked late. I didn't realize anything had happened until I came out to go home."

She pointed toward her two coworkers. "Ruben Jacobs works evenings here at the school, and Lyle Peale is our principal. Detective Kelly arrived right after I first discovered the damage."

She half expected the woman to ask what Jonah was doing there in the first place, but maybe he'd filled her in on the circumstances before she approached Aubrey and the others. She'd ask him later. Right now, all she wanted to do was get this over with and go home.

Mercifully, it didn't take long to give her statement. Officer Goff also took down the contact information for both Ruben and her boss, but that was probably only a formality. When they were done, Ruben asked, "Are you sure you wouldn't like me to change your tire for you?"

Aubrey looked to Jonah for advice before answering. He smiled at the other man. "I'll take care of it, Mr. Jacobs."

Ruben gestured at Jonah's suit. "You're not exactly dressed for getting your hands dirty."

Jonah smiled at him. "That's what dry cleaners are for. Don't worry about it."

While they talked, Lyle sidled closer to her. "Are you sure you're all right?" He glanced toward Jonah. "There's no reason for him to hang around and change the tire for you. I'm sure you have some kind of roadside service coverage. Why don't you call them instead and then wait in my office?"

"Thanks, but I'll be fine. It's just been a long day."

It almost sounded as if there was a hint of snark in Lyle's voice when he mentioned Jonah, but surely not? Like her, he was probably just tired. His day must've been longer than hers, and this time of year was a marathon as everyone rushed to get everything done by the last day of school. Her needing to take a leave of absence had only complicated things for him. To hurry things along, she mustered what she hoped looked like a genuine smile. "I appreciate your concern, but you have more important things to do than babysit me. Jonah can handle the tire. It will take less time for him to do it than having to wait for a tow truck to arrive. I do appreciate you and Ruben coming to my rescue."

At least Lyle didn't argue. "I came back to pick up some papers I need for a meeting at the district office in the morning. I'll go grab them and head out since you have everything under control."

He caught Ruben's eye and jerked his head toward the building. The older man immediately broke off whatever he was saying to Jonah and Officer Goff to follow Lyle up the sidewalk and back toward the building. He stopped only long enough to speak to Aubrey one last time. "If you need anything, even if your fellow needs to wash up after changing the tire, come back into the building. I won't engage the alarm until I know you're gone."

She patted him on the arm. "Thanks, Ruben. We appreciate it."

Officer Goff waited until Ruben was out of hearing before she approached Aubrey. She held out a copy of her report as well as her business card. "I'm sorry this happened, Ms. Sims. Detective Kelly knows how to reach me if you or your insurance company have questions, but you can also call me directly."

"Thank you, and I really appreciate the fast response."

"Any time."

When she was gone, Jonah rejoined Aubrey. "Do you want to wait in my car while I work on the tire?"

"I'll stay with you if that's okay."

"It won't take long." Then his eyes flared wide. "I didn't even think to ask. Do you have a spare?"

For the first time all day, she laughed and held out her keys. "It's in the trunk."

Jonah was still assembling Aubrey's car jack when the school principal came back out. He spoke to Aubrey as he walked by, but barely glanced at Jonah before he got in his car and drove off. Aubrey seemed puzzled by her boss's behavior, but Jonah just shrugged it off. A lot of people were uncomfortable around police officers. Right now, he was more concerned about how well his knee would hold up while he changed the tire. It might end up being one of the nights he'd end up taking a pain pill before bed.

He could have avoided the wear and tear on the joint by accepting Ruben's offer to change the tire. But that might have raised a few questions he didn't want to answer, like why Jonah was taking such care in documenting the damage. As far as Ruben knew, it was just a random act of vandalism, not a serious threat against Aubrey. Jonah wore gloves to preserve any evidence that might be on the spike and the tire itself. Considering how careful Aubrey's stalker had been to date, he didn't hold out much hope. Just in case, he planned to drop everything off in the lab on his way home.

After tightening the lug nuts one last time, he pushed himself back up to his feet and peeled off his gloves. Aubrey held out his suit jacket. "Thanks for doing that for me, but I'm sorry that you've wasted a good part of your evening babysitting me again."

"No apologies necessary." He handed back her keys. "Let's get you home."

Then he checked the time. "Look, I don't know about you, but I'm not going to want to bother cooking tonight. Would you like to stop somewhere to grab a bite before we head to your place?"

"Haven't you had enough of me and my problems for one day? You've already gone above and beyond by changing my tire. You don't need to feed me, too."

She wasn't exactly saying no, but neither was she jumping at the chance to spend more time in his company. He straightened his tie as he considered what he wanted to say. It would be smarter to follow her home, check to make sure everything was as it should be, and then grab a burger on his way home. The truth was that he wanted to spend a little time with Aubrey when they weren't dealing with her case. His reasons behind the invitation were personal, not professional, and therefore it probably wasn't the smartest idea.

Too bad.

"Let's just say that I get tired of eating alone and would appreciate the company."

Aubrey's answering smile was all he could wish for. "Then I'd love to have dinner."

Two hours later, they walked out of a local seafood restaurant, one of Jonah's favorite places in the area. The decor wasn't fancy, but the service was always good and the food excellent. They'd chatted about books, movies and sports. Anything and everything except Aubrey's case and Jonah's job. He didn't know about her, but he'd really enjoyed the chance to simply chill for a while.

Seeing Aubrey so relaxed and happy had given Jonah an enticing glimpse of the woman she could've been all of the time under other circumstances. From the beginning, he'd thought she was pretty, especially with those huge brown eyes and sweet smile. But tonight, the candlelight had emphasized her warm skin and the hints of red in her dark brown hair. They weren't on a date, but it felt like one at times. It was a nice bit of normal, something he hadn't had much of since the night Gino died.

As soon as that guilty thought crossed Jonah's mind, he cringed. How could he have forgotten his friend for even that long? His good mood gone, he instantly snapped right back into cop mode.

"I'll follow you to the house and make sure you get inside safely. I can't hang around, though. I've still got some work to do tonight."

That probably came out harsher than he'd meant it to because Aubrey gave him a confused look. "If you needed to get back to the office, you should've said so sooner. I have work to do, too. I'm also perfectly capable of getting myself back home. It's only a few blocks from here. If you want to know I made it there safely, I could always text you."

"That's not what I meant…"

He realized he was talking to himself. She had already walked away, heading for her car. He thought about catching up with her long enough to apologize, but maybe it was best if he reminded them both that theirs was a business relationship, nothing more. It couldn't be. Not when he needed to concentrate on figuring out who was threatening her.

Rather than chase her down to offer his apology, he decided to wait until they reached her house. He soon got another hint that she wasn't particularly happy with him at the moment. When they approached a traffic light that had already turned yellow, Aubrey punched the gas and scooted through the intersection a hair before the light turned red. He was far enough behind her that he had no choice but to stop. By the time he caught up with her, she was already pulling into her garage.

What was she thinking? They both knew her stalker had been nearby today. If she'd forgotten, he could remind her by showing her the spike in her tire. If the guy had broken into her house while she was gone, he could've been waiting to grab her. Jonah slammed his car door and charged after her before she could close the garage.

From the shock on her face when she got out of the car, she'd been totally oblivious to his approach. "Jonah, you scared me half to death!"

"That's not my fault. You should've been able to see me, considering I walked right down the middle of your driveway and straight into the garage. I didn't hide or sneak in."

He waved his hands in the air. "What if it had been your kidnapper instead of me? If somehow he'd managed to break in, he could have been waiting inside for you. For all the attention you were paying to your surroundings, he could have subdued you in a matter of seconds."

She drew herself up to her full height and glared right back at him as she waved her phone in his face. "I have a security system with cameras in every room. I stopped on the street long enough to check all of the footage. There's no one in the house or the garage."

Not ready to surrender or even admit that he was overreacting, he moved closer, forcing her to tip her head back to look him in the eye. "Fine, I'll give you that much. The point is I came in through the open door, and you weren't watching for a threat in that direction. If he'd gotten you…"

He couldn't complete that thought, but somehow his hands had ended up on her shoulders. Aubrey responded by placing her hands on his chest. He kept his hold gentle, and she didn't push him away. Neither of them said anything for what seemed a long time. Finally, Aubrey said, "I'm sorry, Jonah. You're right. I got careless. I'm sorry for making you worry even more about me. I won't do it again."

"And I'm sorry that I lost my temper." It was time for some honesty. "You know what happened to my partner. I figure you probably understand better than most people what it means to have survivor guilt. When we came out of the restaurant, I realized that it was the first time I'd actually enjoyed myself since the night Gino died. The guilt knocked me sideways for a minute there."

"There's no need to apologize, Jonah. I mean that."

He stared down into her dark eyes as he slowly slid his hands around her, pulling Aubrey in closer, needing this connection. Tucking her head under his chin, he held her lightly, knowing he would let her go the second she wanted him to back off. All he could hope was that she needed this peaceful moment as much as he did. She didn't resist at all, but that didn't stop her from asking, "Jonah, why were we fighting?"

"Stress, probably, even though the last thing I want to do is to fight with you."

"What are we doing now?"

Deciding it was time to go big or go home, he smiled at her. "Probably something else I'll need to apologize for."

Then he kissed her.

ELEVEN

Wow, simply wow. It had been a long, long time since Aubrey had been kissed, but she was pretty sure she'd never experienced anything like this before. Maybe it was because Jonah held her so carefully and treated her with such care. It only lasted a few seconds, but she was pretty sure she would still be feeling the impact for a long time.

Even after she broke off the kiss, Jonah continued to hold her. With her head tucked against his chest, Aubrey sensed he was smiling as he asked, "Well, should I apologize?"

That had her laughing. "Do you hear me complaining?"

"It was unprofessional."

She was caught between him and the car, so she gave him a gentle push to give them each a little room to breathe. "Again, I won't tell if you don't."

"Fair enough, but it probably shouldn't happen again."

"Ever?"

She'd meant that as a small tease, but Jonah evidently took it seriously. "That would be a real shame, but any kind of personal involvement would muddy the waters right now. I need a clear head if I'm going to protect you. And we both know that right now, you're not safe."

The flash of grief in his eyes was a powerful reminder

that he was still dealing with the loss of his friend. Logic said that neither of them was at fault for what had happened to Marta or Gino, but they both still carried a burden of guilt from their loss.

She reached up to cup Jonah's cheek. "Then we'll revisit this moment when it's safe. Until then, we should place our trust in God to see us both through this. With His help, we'll both find peace and safety."

Jonah closed his eyes as he leaned into her touch. "Amen, Aubrey. Amen."

Then he stepped back. "We should get you inside. We both have work to do."

She closed the garage door and let Jonah lead the way into the house. Once they were in the kitchen, she entered the code on the security system while Jonah did a quick scan of the kitchen, dining room and living room. "I'm sorry if it feels like I'm invading your privacy, but I should check the bedrooms, too."

Having someone else go through her house like this wasn't comfortable, but she knew she should let him do it for his peace of mind, as well as hers. "Do whatever you need to do."

He was back within a few minutes. "Everything looks good. Is there anything else you'd like me to do before I leave?"

"No, I'm good."

"What time are you leaving for work in the morning? I'll come here, then follow you."

She hated to ask him to do that but suspected she had little choice in the matter. "I have to be there by eight o'clock, so we should leave by seven thirty."

"Got it. If I can't make it for some reason, I'll text you and ask a patrol officer to do the honors instead."

Aubrey unlocked the front door for him. "I guess I'll see you in the morning."

He brushed a lock of her hair back away from her face. "Call if you need me."

"I will."

She watched and waved from the front window until he drove away.

The next morning, Jonah arrived at the diner twenty minutes late. He paused right inside the door to scan the crowd for George Swahn. As soon as he spotted him, he wended his way through the cluster of tables and chairs to a booth in the back next to the window.

"Sorry I'm late. I followed Aubrey Sims to school first, and traffic was worse than I expected."

George had been about to take a drink of his coffee, but he set the mug back down on the table with a thud. "What's happened now?"

Their server appeared before Jonah could answer. They waited to continue the conversation until after they'd given their orders. As soon as they were alone, Jonah launched into a summary of what had happened since they'd last spoken.

By the time he'd finished catching him up, George was looking pretty grim. "This guy is ramping up fast."

Jonah nodded. "Yeah. He's locked in on Aubrey as his target, but he's not ready to make his final move quite yet. It's impossible to know why that is. Maybe he gets off on having all of us running in circles or knowing that Aubrey is living in fear, never knowing when he'll strike again."

George had been taking notes, probably out of habit from when he'd been on active duty. He looked up from his notebook. "And the lab hasn't been able to pick up anything useful from the original note, the coin or the spike?"

"Not so far. They didn't get the tire until late yesterday, so I doubt they'd have had a chance to get to it as yet. I'm not holding out much hope, though."

"How is Aubrey holding up? This has to be taking a toll on her."

Jonah stared out the window, not wanting to look at the other man in case his expression would reveal more than he wanted it to. "She's stronger than she looks. It's amazing she's doing as well as she is considering how little support she's had from her family over the years."

"What makes you say that?"

"Her parents were furious when I first showed up at their house to review the facts of the original incident in light of the new threat. They actually ordered me not to reopen the case and to stay away from their daughter. I happened to be at Aubrey's house later that day when they showed up. They can't understand why she can't simply forget about what happened and move on. They won't even let themselves believe there is any reason for concern. It's like hiding their heads in the sand is the only way they can cope with any of this."

That encounter hadn't been fun for any of them, but he couldn't help but admire the way Aubrey had stood up to her parents. "Aubrey fought back and then ordered them out of her house for insulting me. Like I said, she's stronger than she looks."

Their food arrived, interrupting their conversation again. Jonah took a few bites and then set down his fork.

"I also talked to Ross Easton and the Pynes. Did you know that Ross used to stalk Aubrey?"

George looked up. "Seriously? She never mentioned that to me. Could he be behind this?"

"I don't think so. He's gotten sober in the interim. He also didn't strike me as the kind of guy who would be an accomplished liar. When I told him there was a new threat to Aubrey, he seemed genuinely shocked and angry."

They stopped talking long enough to finish their meals. As they relaxed and drank their coffee, Jonah said, "It wasn't easy, but at least I've convinced Aubrey to take a leave of absence for the rest of the school year. She really wanted to finish out the last week with her students. I think she might have been having second thoughts about taking off work until she saw the tire last night. Knowing he followed her to school pretty much clinched the deal. I suggested she stay with her parents, but that was a definite no-go."

George briefly grinned. "I've always known she was stubborn. Most people would've given up looking for answers years ago."

"True enough. Did you know she hired multiple private investigators over the years to look into the case?"

"Yeah, although she never told me herself. A couple were former cops themselves and reached out to talk to me about the case. As far as I know, none of them found anything useful."

"She gave me the files, but I haven't had a chance to read through all of them yet. What I have read is pretty much what we already knew."

"I could read the rest of them for you, or anything else

that might help. My wife's out of town visiting her sister for a week, so I'm free."

That was just what Jonah had been hoping for. There were only so many hours in the day, and his gut feeling was that the hours before this guy struck again were ticking down rapidly. "That would be great. I've also been doing searches for similar cases over the past twelve years. Nothing local fits, so I need to search farther afield. I talked to the captain yesterday, and he said it was okay if I brought you on board if you were interested."

"I'm in. Did you learn anything new from talking to Easton or Marta's parents?"

Jonah flipped back through his own notes. "Yeah, actually I did. It's likely nothing, but their stories don't line up on one small detail. I asked Ross what he could remember about what the girls were involved in back then, other than going to class. He mentioned that Marta had a job at the college library she would have had to quit at the end of the term because she was leaving to study abroad. But when I went over the same info with her folks, they insisted she'd already left her job before she was abducted. Evidently something happened that caused her to quit sooner than expected, but why Ross wouldn't have known or remembered that, I don't know."

George frowned. "Funny, I don't remember anyone mentioning any of that in the original reports."

"They didn't. Maybe there's nothing to it, but it makes me wonder how they missed it."

"Does Aubrey know anything about it?"

Chagrined, Jonah shrugged. "I haven't asked her. With everything that's happened, I haven't had a chance. I will when I see her later today."

* * *

Back at the station, they got started on the files Aubrey had given Jonah. For the most part, they didn't contain anything that they didn't already know. Frustrating, but not surprising.

Jonah stood up and stretched. "I need to walk around a little to stretch my leg."

George gave him a considering look. "How's the knee?"

"Actually, better than I thought it would be, especially after changing Aubrey's tire last night." He picked up his coffee mug. "I'm going to go top off my coffee. Want some?"

"Sure. One sugar, no creamer."

When Jonah returned, George was leaning back in his chair, his fingers entwined behind his head as he stared up at the ceiling. "I've been thinking about what happened in that parking lot. It could've been a random act, but I don't think so. Not when that's how the original kidnapper immobilized Aubrey's car twelve years ago."

He glanced at Jonah. "Here's the thing. The original investigators were pretty much split down the middle on whether the guy picked those two girls at random or if he'd gone after one or both of them for a specific reason. Without any proof either way, that line of investigation never went anywhere."

"But you're thinking that if the same guy has spiked Aubrey's tire again, either she or Marta was probably targeted. If so, he probably hung around last night in case he could grab Aubrey again while no one was around."

George sat up straight again. "Yeah, seems likely. The question is, how did he know that she would work later than usual yesterday? Because even if he'd somehow managed to sabotage her tire during the day without being seen, there would have been too many people around to snatch her out of the parking lot if she'd left at her regular time."

Jonah sat down and rubbed his aching leg. "What's more, he also couldn't have known that she'd have someone watching her as she left the building, or that I was coming to follow her home."

"Well, unless he was watching from somewhere close by."

"The school is on a side street, but it's only a block or so away from the main drag. Most of the staff get off work by four o'clock, and Aubrey left the building a little after six. That means the tire was most likely slashed in between those hours. I'll see if there's any traffic cameras in that area and get any video that covers that time period."

"Good idea. If you do manage to get video, let me know. That's something else I can help with."

"Not that I'm not grateful for the assistance, but didn't you retire to get away from all this?"

If anything, the other man looked even more determined. "I told you before I left that certain cases will hit you harder, especially the ones where you never get justice for the victims. This is one of them."

He paused to point at some of the other files on Jonah's desk. "If we can finally catch the guy who did this, I'm thinking it will make it easier for me to live with all those other unsolved cases. That's because it will give me hope someone, someday will find the answers for those, too. The bottom line is that I'm yours as long as you need me."

"Fair enough."

Jonah understood all too well what George was telling him. He was also thankful for the older man's advice. He'd been praying for God's guidance ever since Gino died. Maybe He had led Jonah to cross paths with both George and Aubrey, knowing having them in his life would help ease the burden of Gino's death. He liked to think so.

He checked the time. "I'll need to leave in half an hour to follow Aubrey home from work. I'm not sure how long I'll be gone."

"No sweat. If I run across anything important, I'll call you. Tell Aubrey that I said hi."

"I will."

The day had been a long one. The kids in her class had been upset when she explained that it was going to be their last day with her as their teacher. At least the sub who had been assigned to the class was familiar to them. Mrs. Denisi had come in to spend the afternoon with Aubrey and her students to help smooth the transition. Between the two of them, they'd finished the day's lessons with enough time left over for a small goodbye party. Aubrey hadn't wanted to stop at the store on the way to work, so she'd had some treats delivered to the office.

The kids and Mrs. Denisi had left for the day, leaving Aubrey alone to finish a few odds and ends before locking up. She'd already texted Jonah to say she was ready to go home.

She locked up and headed for the office to check in with the school secretary and Principal Peale, if he was available. Viola came around the counter to hug Aubrey. "When things settle down, we'll get together for coffee. I'll expect a full explanation as to how you met that good-looking guy you've been keeping secret from me."

It still hurt to lie to her friend, but there was no way

she wanted to entangle anyone else in her situation. "Give me a couple of weeks. I'll even spring for some of those chocolate pastries you like so much."

"It's a deal."

Aubrey nodded toward Lyle's office. "Is he around? I wanted to check in with him on my way out."

"No, he's at the district office. You know how it is at this time of the year. Nothing but meeting after meeting. I'll let him know that you tried."

Viola stopped to glance through the window that faced the school entrance. Her expression turned a bit wicked. "Speaking of your fellow, he just walked into the building. I have to admire your taste in men. Such bright blue eyes and that blond hair...not to mention those broad shoulders. He's a real cutie. It makes me wish I was twenty years younger and single."

Aubrey snickered. "You're not wrong about him, but you've got your own guy. You'd never trade David in for another model."

"No, I wouldn't, and I'm grateful for each and every one of the thirty years we've had together. Now, you get going. Don't keep the man waiting."

"See you soon."

Aubrey joined Jonah out in the hall. "Thanks for coming inside. I have to admit that I was a bit reluctant to walk out to the parking lot alone today."

"No problem. I thought you might need help carrying all your stuff out to the car since it's your last day."

"It's already in my trunk. I got a couple of friends to help carry everything out during lunch today."

As they walked out and started toward the parking lot, he studied their surroundings, watching for any possible threats. He paused to give her a sympathetic look. "I know turning your class over to someone else is probably hard for you, but it really is the best thing for both you and your class under the circumstances."

"I know. At least it's almost summer anyway, and it helps knowing that I'll be back in the fall."

"That makes sense." He glanced at her again. "By the way, George Swahn asked me to say hi for him. He and I had breakfast this morning after I followed you to work. Then he insisted on coming into the office to go through the files you gave me."

She winced. "Is that going to get him in trouble with Mrs. Swahn?"

"I wondered the same thing, but evidently she's out of town visiting her sister."

They'd reached her car. Before letting her get near it, Jonah did a quick inspection to make sure there weren't any more unpleasant surprises. "All clear."

"Good. I'll see you at the house?"

"Yep, and I'll check inside the house for you again."

"I appreciate it," she said, allowing her gaze to linger on his face for a second too long. She mentally checked herself and got into her car before he could see the blush rapidly spreading across her cheeks.

Once they got to her place, Jonah made good on his promise to do a quick walk-through of the house. After he gave it the all clear, it took them several trips to carry everything she'd brought home from school inside. She dumped all of it on the dining room table to sort through later after Jonah left. It would give her something to do other than worry.

As soon as he drove away, she did her own inspection. It wasn't as if she didn't think he'd done a thorough job, but old habits died hard. As soon as she'd reassured herself that all was as it should be, she went online and ordered groceries. She was low on a few things, and she'd promised Jonah she'd handle her errands remotely as much as possible.

With that done, there was one more thing to take care of before she settled in for the evening. She had a few flowerpots on the front porch and a couple on the small patio in the back that needed watering; the sprinkler system took care of the rest.

She waved at her neighbors as she watered the plants in front. Since there were several people within sight, she took advantage of the opportunity to spend a little more time outside pulling a few weeds. She had just finished when her phone rang. Seeing it was her mother, she answered it as she let herself back into the house.

"Hi, Mom. What's up?"

"Dad and I haven't seen you since…well, when we had to cut the visit short. We've missed you and were wondering if you'd like to come over for dinner one night next week after you get off work."

Heading for the bathroom to wash her hands, Aubrey considered how much, if anything, she should tell her folks about what was really going on. The truth would only upset them, but she thought it would hurt them even more to learn that she was keeping secrets from them—especially the potentially life-threatening kind.

"I'm not sure that's a good idea, Mom."

Nothing but silence.

"Mom?"

"What's happened now, Aubrey?"

She hated the fear in her mother's voice. "First of all, I'm fine, and Detective Kelly is working hard to make sure I stay that way," she said as she washed her hands in the sink, the cell phone tucked between her shoulder and her ear. "With that in mind, we decided I should take a few precautions. He suggested I stick close to home as much as possible, so I've taken a leave of absence from school. I'll be temporarily ordering my groceries online. Stuff like that."

That went over as well as she had expect it to, judging by the anger in her mother's voice. "Which means there's more going on than you've bothered to tell us."

Aubrey dried her hands and walked back into her bedroom, wishing she had easy answers for her mother that wouldn't set off another firestorm. But as she was debating what to say next, she saw something that made her heart turn over in her chest. She took a step closer the window on the far wall to make sure of what she was seeing and then went into full panic.

Someone had paid her another visit, this time armed with a can of spray paint.

"Look, Mom, something's just come up. I need to hang up, but I'll try to call you later."

Her poor mother was still sputtering in protest as Aubrey disconnected the call. Meanwhile, her knees were shaking so badly that she had to lean against the wall for support as she called Jonah, counting the seconds until he answered.

"Aubrey, what's happened?"

"He left me another message. Spray-painted it on the outside of my bedroom window. The words were written backwards, so I could read them from inside. The paint is still dripping down the glass."

"What's it say?"

"You can run, but you can't hide."

"I'm on my way."

TWELVE

Jonah showed his injured knee no mercy as he charged out of his office with George Swahn hot on his heels. He'd already sent a patrol officer to stay with Aubrey until he could get there himself. That was the only reason he stopped long enough to update his boss on the current situation while George waited outside in the hall. Captain Martine was on the phone when he walked in. He took one look at Jonah's face and hung up.

"Sir, something's happened at Aubrey Sims's place again. Slashing her tire at the school where she works was bad enough. Now he's left her another threatening message written in spray paint on the outside of her bedroom window. It had to have happened after I followed her home. We need to get her into protective custody."

His boss was looking pretty grim. "I agree. This guy isn't going to be content to keep playing games for much longer. You go check on Ms. Sims while I call the county and see if we can use one of their safe houses. If one isn't available, I'll figure something out. At the very least I'll assign an officer to watch her house around the clock until we can get her moved."

"Thank you, sir."

Jonah walked out of the captain's office and leaned against the wall. The news that they'd finally be able to put her in protective custody allowed him to draw a full breath of air for the first time since he'd answered Aubrey's call. George stood nearby without speaking, probably giving Jonah a chance to get his bearings. When Jonah finally stood up straight again, George got right back to business.

"I probably shouldn't go to Aubrey's with you since I'm not on active duty. If it's okay with you, I'll stay here and keep looking through the files. The traffic cam video should be cued up soon. I can start scanning through that if it would help. Any ideas as to who or what I should be looking for?"

"Not really."

Which was one of the biggest frustrations in this case. Regardless, they had to start somewhere. "I'm almost positive that Ross Easton isn't our guy, but watch for his vehicle. The make of his car and the plate number is already in the file. While you're at it, there's a janitor at her school named Ruben something… Ruben Jacobs, that's it. See if you can track down the info on his vehicle, as well as her principal's."

George looked surprised. "Do you have any reason to think either of them might be our guy?"

"No, but both of them had opportunity to spike her tire. We won't catch that on the film, but maybe the janitor arrived earlier than normal or something. The principal had already left the building before Aubrey did, but he came back right when she discovered the damage. Again, that doesn't really mean anything, but it could. It might also be worth checking to see if they were at the school at the time the paint was sprayed on her house."

He started walking toward the elevator. "We've got nothing concrete to go on, so I think it's too early to eliminate anyone. What really bothers me is that Aubrey doesn't seem to have many men in her life. Even most of her coworkers are women. And from what she's told me, it's been ages since she's even dated anyone. But whoever this guy is, he's watching her from somewhere close. We need answers."

George visibly shuddered. "I'll do my best to find them. We both will."

Jonah met the other man's gaze. "I know. The question is if our best will be enough."

Then he walked away, praying for all he was worth that they wouldn't run out of time before they were able to close in on the person who was doing this.

The trip from the precinct to Aubrey's house wasn't long by distance, but Jonah couldn't get there fast enough. Stopping to talk to his captain had been necessary, but it only added to the time Aubrey had to wait for Jonah to arrive. He knew the responding officer would do their best to reassure her, but it wasn't the same. That was *his* job, not just as the officer in charge but because…well, just because.

As he pulled up in front of her house, he groaned when he saw the car parked in Aubrey's driveway. What were her parents doing there? It didn't seem likely that she would have asked them to come running. As far as he knew, she hadn't been keeping them in the loop about everything that had happened, especially since they'd made it clear that neither of them wanted to know why her case had heated up again.

One of the patrol officers was just coming around the side of the garage from the backyard. He was relieved to see it was April Goff, who had also responded when Aubrey's tire was slashed at the school. She headed straight for him. "No wonder you took the tire thing at the school so seriously. That message written on the window is big-time scary."

"So I hear. I thought I'd check it out before I talk to Ms. Sims."

"By the way, Ms. Sims is inside with her parents. I swear you could cut the tension between them with a knife. I offered to stay with her until you got here, but she asked me to keep watch outside." Then Officer Goff frowned. "Did I do the right thing? Because I got the distinct impression she was protecting me rather than the other way around."

He didn't doubt that for a second. "It's fine. I've crossed paths with her parents before, and it wasn't any fun, especially for Aubrey. Like I told you at the school, she was kidnapped twelve years ago. We think whoever is behind the tire and the paint is likely the same guy. Her parents don't want to believe any of it is real, because that would mean she's in danger again."

His assessment of the situation clearly shocked his co-worker. "Do they actually think denial will make the danger disappear?"

"Honestly, I'm not sure. I keep reminding myself that everyone handles stress and fear in their own way." He fisted his hands in frustration. "If they're not happy now, I can only imagine how they're going to react when we put her in protective custody and cut her off completely from any outside contact."

Officer Goff shook her head. "I'm glad dealing with all of that is above my pay grade."

There wasn't much he could say to that. "If you'll keep

watch out front, I want to see the paint job before I go inside. If the forensics team shows up, send them on back."

"Will do."

He walked around to the backyard, needing to see this
new threat for himself. After taking a close look at the
words on Aubrey's window, Jonah slipped on a glove and
touched the paint. Just as Aubrey had said, it wasn't completely dry, meaning the guy had been there right after
Jonah had done his walk-through of the house. His initial
reaction was pure fury and left him wishing there was
something he could punch. Anything to vent some of his
anger. It would help clear his head before he had to deal
with Aubrey and her parents. He would need all the control he could muster to maintain some distance from her
when his instincts were shouting at him to comfort her and
reassure himself that she was all right. Maybe having her
parents there to chaperone might not be such a bad thing.

He took a few pictures of the backwards writing. After
forwarding one to George, he shoved his phone in his
pocket as he took a slow walk around the perimeter of
the yard. The cedar fence was six feet tall, pretty typical
for the area. Along the way, he stood on his toes to look
over into each of the neighbors' yards. It was impossible
to tell if her stalker had entered the yard from one of the
others, but maybe the forensics people would see something he'd missed.

He hoped so. They needed a break in this case in the
worst way.

After he'd done everything he could, it was time to go
inside. Bracing himself for what might be another ugly
confrontation with Mr. and Mrs. Sims, he knocked on the
door. "Aubrey, it's me."

He listened to the all-too-familiar sound of her going through the complicated process of unlocking the door. When she finally opened it, he was both relieved and disappointed that she quickly backed away to give him room to enter her house. Apparently, he wasn't the only one who realized they needed to maintain professional decorum in front of her parents.

"Detective Kelly, thank you for coming."

"Sorry it took me so long. I had to update my captain on the case before I came." He looked past her to where her parents stood glaring at him from the living room and nodded to acknowledge their presence. "Mr. and Mrs. Sims."

When her mother started to speak, he cut her off. "I need to talk to your daughter."

Without giving the woman a chance to respond, he turned back to Aubrey. "Before coming inside, I went around to the back to take pictures of the message, but I also need to take pictures of it from inside. Would you mind showing me the way?"

Aubrey raised her eyebrows, probably surprised that he was acting as if he hadn't been over every square inch of her house by this point. "Sure, come this way."

Her father planted himself in front of the hallway, blocking their path. "I'll go with you. Aubrey can stay here with her mother."

Jonah considered asking him to step aside, but the man was feeling understandably protective of his daughter. Rather than argue, he shrugged. "Okay."

When Aubrey started to protest, he shook his head. "It's fine, Aubrey. This won't take long."

Mr. Sims remained silent until they reached Aubrey's bedroom. When he raised the blinds to reveal the message,

Jonah had no idea if it was the other man's first time seeing it or not. Regardless, his reaction was fierce. "What kind of sicko terrorizes a woman like this? And why haven't you put a stop to it by now?"

Jonah didn't take the man's anger personally. Besides, he was right to be concerned about the lack of progress on the case. "I promise you that we're working on it, Mr. Sims. Whoever is behind these stunts has done a good job of covering his tracks. We are pursuing every avenue of inquiry we can."

"That's not good enough."

Jonah would have protested, but he actually agreed with the man's assessment of the situation. "No, sir, it's not. I'm not making excuses, but it's like he's a ghost. He didn't make any mistakes twelve years ago, and he hasn't this time, either. At least not so far."

Aubrey's father lowered the blinds but made no move to leave the room. "I hate this for Aubrey. It's no surprise that what happened last time changed her. I can't stand the thought of her living in fear again."

Did he actually think she'd ever really stopped? Not that Jonah was going to ask him that. If Aubrey's parents hadn't figured out the significance of all those locks on the door and the expensive security system, he wasn't going to explain it to them. "I'm done in here."

Mr. Sims led the way back to the front of the house where his daughter and his wife still stood on opposite sides of the room, neither of them looking happy. Aubrey met Jonah's gaze. "What do you think?"

He wanted to tell her that it was no big deal, but he wouldn't lie to her. "That he's upped the ante again. I've already talked to my captain. He's working out the details to move you to a safe house."

"That's it!" Her mother pointed at her daughter. "Pack a bag. You're moving back home right now."

Aubrey all but rolled her eyes at her mother's attempt to bully her into meek compliance. "Sorry, Mom, but that's not going to happen."

It was clear which of her parents Aubrey had inherited her stubborn determination from as her mother puffed up in outrage. For a brief second, Jonah felt a little sympathy for her father for having to deal with two such strong personalities.

On the other hand, it was interesting that Mr. Sims remained at the entrance to the hallway rather than positioning himself next to either his wife or his daughter. Was he trying to remain neutral rather than choose sides? If so, Jonah had serious doubts that it was going to play out well for the man. Sure enough, his wife shot him an angry look. "Tell her, Joe. It's the only sensible option."

"I'm sorry, Sandy, but I can't do that. As Aubrey reminded us last time we were here, she's an adult and entitled to make her own decisions." He held up his hand when his wife started to protest. "Listen to what I'm trying to tell you. If Aubrey chooses to follow Detective Kelly's advice, it's not because she doesn't love us. It means she wants us to be safe, too. She doesn't want to bring her troubles to our doorstep."

Jonah wasn't sure who was more shocked by Joe's assessment of the situation—his daughter or his wife—but he admired the guy for understanding what his daughter was going through. Aubrey hurried to her father's side and gave him a huge hug. He patted her on the back and asked, "It's why you took the rest of the year off from school, isn't it?"

She nodded. "He knows where I work. He spiked my tire in the school parking lot. I can't be there and risk him doing something to harm the kids or my friends."

As Aubrey explained the situation to her father, Jonah watched her mother's reaction. He might not always like the way the woman talked to her daughter, he didn't doubt for a second that her intentions were good. She knew full well how close they'd come to losing Aubrey twelve years ago and lived in terror of it happening again. Everything that had happened since the note and coin appeared in Aubrey's mailbox was her parents' worst nightmare coming to life.

Jonah approached her. "Are you all right, Mrs. Sims?"

Her eyes snapped up to meet his gaze. "No, I'm not all right. Nothing about this is *all right*. I can't go through this again. None of us can."

"I will do my best to make sure your daughter is safe. That's all anyone can promise."

Then he pulled a worn card from his wallet and handed it to her. "My pastor gave this to me when I hit a rough patch a couple of months back. Whenever things get to be more than I can handle alone, I read it. I've found it helpful. Maybe you will as well."

She took the card and read it aloud. Her voice started off unsteady, but grew in strength as she reached the end of the verse. "*Be strong and courageous. Do not fear or be in dread of them, for it is the LORD your God who goes with you. He will not leave you or forsake you. Deuteronomy 31:6.*"

Several tears trickled down her cheek. "Thank you, Detective Kelly."

When she started to hand the card back, he shook his head. "Keep it for now, Mrs. Sims. You can give it back when all of this is over with."

She managed a small nod and then crossed the room to join her husband and daughter. "I apologize for ordering you around again, Aubrey. We'll support your decision no matter what you decide to do. I know you're trying to protect everyone around you, including us. Just remember, the only thing that matters to us is that you're safe."

Aubrey hugged her mother, her own eyes looking a bit shiny with tears. "We can't control whatever this crazy guy does, Mom. All we can do is make the best decisions we can under the circumstances. No matter what happens next, know that I love you as much as you love me."

While they continued to talk, Jonah went into the kitchen and fixed himself a glass of water. He was sure that Aubrey wouldn't mind, and it would give her and her parents a little privacy. There was no telling how long it would be before they saw each other again, and they deserved a chance to make peace with each other.

It wasn't long before the front door opened and closed, leaving a heavy silence in the house. Jonah set down his glass and went in search of Aubrey. He found her at the front window, peeking out through the blinds as her parents got in their car and drove away.

"It's hard not to think this might have been the last time I'll see them. I think they're worried about the same thing—that no matter how careful we are, no matter how we try, he's going to find me."

All of Jonah's resolve to maintain an emotional distance from Aubrey until she was safe from the current threat to her life went by the wayside. He tugged her back from the window as soon as her parents were out of sight and wrapped her in his arms. "We can't lose faith, Aubrey. We'll figure this out and bring him to justice. Then you and your family can finally have closure. Marta's parents and Ross, too."

She rested against his chest, her arms around his waist. "It's hard to believe that will happen, even though I've prayed it would every day for twelve years."

"There is strength in numbers, Aubrey, and you're not alone. You have so many people working to put an end to this. Right now, even though he's retired, George Swahn is at headquarters going through all the files and the video from cameras near the school looking for anything that will point us in the right direction. We're all praying for this to end."

She sniffled a bit, but then took a step back with renewed determination. "So, what are you hoping to find in my files that everyone else has missed over the years?"

Jonah didn't want to get her hopes up, but it might help her to know that they had found at least one small string to tug on. "We've already found one anomaly. It might not be anything, but it's a start."

"What kind of anomaly?"

Noticing how pale she was, he suggested, "Why don't you sit down while I fix us something to drink, and maybe grab a few cookies if there are any left?"

It said a lot that she gave in to his suggestion so easily. "Help yourself. I baked more."

When he returned a few minutes later, she was sitting at the dining room table, staring at nothing in particular. He handed her a cup of tea and set his own in front of the chair next to hers. He returned to the kitchen to get the cookies before settling in next to her. When she picked up her tea, he started talking.

"We know that Marta worked in the school library. When I talked to Ross, he said she was going to have to quit her job to study abroad."

"Yeah, that's right. She was so excited about the chance to live in England for a semester."

"But here's the thing—her parents said she'd already quit. They thought something might have happened there that she didn't like. Did she mention anything like that to you, do you remember?"

Aubrey leaned back in her chair and briefly closed her eyes. After a few seconds, she frowned and looked at him. "Yeah, maybe. She came home from work one night really mad about some guy. I guess he'd gotten handsy. I asked if she told Ross about it, but Marta said she'd taken care of the problem herself. I think maybe she was worried that Ross might go after the guy, but now that I think about it, she did quit working there not long afterward. I thought it was because she needed more time to get through finals and to make sure she had all her paperwork in order to leave the country."

Jonah set his tea aside so he could take notes. "I know it was a long time ago, but did she mention his name? Was he a student at the college, or did he happen to work at the library, too?"

"Honestly, I don't remember, but it happened three or maybe four weeks before we were kidnapped. Long enough that I doubt I would've thought to tell the police about it when they asked if anything unusual had recently happened to either one of us. You would think that if the guy had continued to be a problem, she would have said something or acted like something was bothering her. As far as I can remember, she was her usual self, all bubbly about leaving for England, but also about getting engaged to Ross."

That was probably true. If Marta had quit because of the incident, she might have thought that had put an end to the matter. The question was if the mystery guy had felt the same. Jonah planned to request a list of the library staff from the time the kidnapping took place. Of course, that would only help if he had actually worked at the library.

Still, at this point in time, any lead at all was worth pursuing.

His phone chimed to announce an incoming text. "It's my captain. He wants me to call him. Hopefully he's managed to line up a safe place for you to stay. Why don't you go pack enough clothes for a few days while I get the details?"

She set her tea back on the table and headed for her bedroom. Right before she would have disappeared from his sight, she stopped and looked back. "I hate this, Jonah. I really do."

He offered her a sympathetic smile. "It's probably no comfort, but so do I."

THIRTEEN

Sergeant Decker walked into the conference room without knocking. "Hey, Jonah, I think this is the fax you've been looking for. It's from the college."

Jonah held out his hand. "Thanks, Tim. It took them long enough."

"You're welcome." Decker started to leave, but stopped to ask, "Can I get you guys anything?"

George leaned back in his seat and stretched his arms. "A new set of eyes and a more comfortable chair would be nice."

Jonah huffed a small laugh. "While you're at it, how about a masseuse?"

Decker grinned and held up his hands. "Sorry, guys, but that's not happening. I might be able to swing some fresh coffee and a couple of sandwiches, though."

Jonah reached for his wallet and pulled out three twenties and a five. "Get something for yourself, too. Anything is fine, but my first choice would be a Philly cheesesteak. George?"

"That sounds good. My wife tries to limit how much red meat I eat, so I'm loading up on it while she's gone."

"I'll get right on it." Decker took the money. "By the

way, the captain wants an update before you guys stop for the night."

"Will do."

Not that Jonah planned on leaving anytime soon. Besides, they didn't have much to report. George was still watching the traffic cam footage from the area around the school. They'd expanded their request to the area around Aubrey's house, as well. So far, they'd netted a whole bunch of nothing.

"I can finish looking at the traffic stuff, George. You should head home and get some rest. You didn't retire in order to end up back here working eighteen hours a day without pay."

"Hey, I'm getting a free sandwich. Saves me cooking when I get home. I'll probably leave after we eat, but I'll be back first thing in the morning."

There was no use convincing him that he'd already done enough, so Jonah didn't bother trying. Besides, he appreciated the help. Then George surprised him with his next comment. "You should go home and get some rest, too. You've been working pretty much around the clock. Keep that up, and eventually you'll crash and won't be much good for anything."

Jonah looked at the piles of paper on the table. "I want to get through this stuff plus the list the college sent over first."

Jonah made a show of studying one of the reports, but the ploy didn't work. George immediately leaned back in his chair and crossed his arms over his chest. "So, how is Aubrey holding up? I know she's only been at the safe house since yesterday evening, but I can't imagine that it's been easy for her."

Jonah picked up the fax from the university and started

flipping through the pages. Seeing how many names were listed only made his head hurt. "She's doing better than expected, but she's already bored out of her mind."

"No surprise there. Are you going to stop by to check on her?"

"Hadn't planned on it. I've called her a couple of times, though. You know, just to keep in touch and to see if she needs anything."

George nodded as if that confirmed something he'd been thinking. "You like her, don't you?"

Where was George going with this? Jonah kept his focus on the papers in front of him as he answered, "She's a nice woman. But even if she wasn't, she deserves to live without having to look over her shoulder all the time."

His companion snorted in response. "That's the cop talking. I'm asking the man."

Jonah gave up all pretense of working. "What exactly are you saying?"

"This case has really gotten to you. I'm wondering why."

His temper stirred to life. "What do you expect? Am I supposed to not care so much? We both know the clock is ticking. If I don't get this figured out, Aubrey could very well die. That can't happen, not on my watch."

He drew a shuddering breath. "Not again."

"So this isn't just about Aubrey, or at least not only her." George sighed. "You have to get it through your head that you weren't at fault for Gino's death, Jonah. Don't shoulder the blame for something you didn't do and couldn't control. If you can't set all of that aside, you're in the wrong job."

"You weren't there that night, George. I was." The images of what had happened immediately played out in his head, just as they had so many times before—the pain, the blood, his best friend's death. "Gino died in my arms. How am I supposed to set that aside?"

The sympathy in the other man's eyes was almost his undoing. "By being the best cop you know how to be. That means focusing on the case in front of you, and forgetting about everything else until you solve it."

He held up his hand when Jonah would have interrupted him. "I'm not saying that it's easy, especially because Gino wasn't just another cop. You have every right to grieve for the loss of your friend, but what you can't do is let his death destroy you. He wouldn't want that to happen, and you know it."

George paused, probably to let that much sink in. "We're doing everything we can to protect Aubrey and to get this guy, but we're only human. We'll work until Decker comes back with our sandwiches. Then we'll eat, pack up and go home. After a few hours' sleep, we'll look at everything with fresh eyes."

George wasn't wrong, especially since Captain Martine had given him the same lecture earlier that afternoon. He'd pointed out that Jonah wasn't alone in handling the case. Even if George hadn't volunteered to assist, they had the forensics team reviewing both the new evidence and everything from twelve years ago. Then there was the team of uniformed officers watching the safe house. The list went on and on.

"Fine. Dinner and then home."

"Smart man."

Jonah had already talked to Aubrey twice that day, but he couldn't resist the temptation to call one more time. She answered on the second ring. "Hey, there."

"Did I call too late? I didn't mean to wake you up."

Her laughter came through loud and clear. "It's only nine o'clock. I'm a big girl. My mommy and daddy let me stay up later than that these days."

"Very funny. I've sort of lost track of time. I thought it was later than that."

After a short hesitation, Aubrey asked, "When is the last time you actually slept?"

"Actually, I'm not sure. Considering how foggy my brain is right now, I guess it's been a while."

"Tell me you're not still at the office. Because if you are, I'm going to hang up so you can drag yourself home to get some serious shut-eye."

That she was concerned about his well-being probably shouldn't make him so happy, but it did. "I am home and about to crash for the night. I wanted to make sure you're doing all right."

Her voice softened. "I'm fine. Well, mostly. You know how it is. I can voluntarily spend days at home alone with no problem. But tell me I can't go anywhere, and I instantly get claustrophobic."

"That sounds about right. Do you need more books or anything?"

"No, I have several left to read. I've also been watching some television. Mostly old sitcoms and ball games. Doesn't matter who is playing. I like the background noise while I read."

"Maybe we should take in a game together one of these days."

The invitation slipped out before he thought about the implications. All things considered, he shouldn't be asking her out on a date. "Look, forget I said that. We should probably write it off to me being too tired to think straight."

"So, are you apologizing for asking me out on a date because you don't want to see a game with me at all? Or is it because you can't date someone you're dealing with in the course of your job?"

"The second one. Definitely not the first."

"Good answer. We'll put the game on hold for the time being. Now, you'd better call it a night before you get yourself into any more trouble."

"Fair enough."

"One more thing, Jonah."

"Yeah?"

"No matter how this turns out, I'm glad I met you. I thank God every day for bringing you into my life."

"Right back at you. I'll call you tomorrow."

"I'm already counting the hours. Now get some sleep."

The line went silent, which was disappointing. Just talking to her eased his worry. However, right now they'd both be better off if he slept a few hours and got back to work. Before drifting off, he did his own fair share of praying— for Aubrey, and asking His guidance on how to end this nightmare for good.

After only two days, Aubrey had memorized every square inch of the tiny, run-down safe house. The only saving grace was that someone had been thoughtful enough to spring for more than basic cable. Considering she couldn't go outside, her only choice of entertainment was either reading or watching television.

She was about to check what time the baseball game was going to start when there was a knock at the front door. She glanced at the time on the cable box. Just as she suspected, it was time for a shift change. After checking through the peephole, she opened the door, happy to recognize Officer Goff. She was Aubrey's favorite of her rotating crew of guardians.

"Hi, Aubrey. I wanted to let you know I was here. An officer friend of mine just texted and offered to drop off dinner for me this evening. Would you like me to order something for you as well? And do you like Italian?"

Anything was better than the frozen dinners the house had come stocked with. "I'll have whatever you're having if it isn't too much trouble. I've got some cash with me, so I can pay you back."

"Don't worry about it. He said he'd make the delivery around six or so."

"That sounds great. It will be a nice change to my routine." She smiled at the other woman. "I know I can't offer you any wine, but I have soft drinks, coffee and tea."

"Sounds good. I'll knock when the food arrives."

"I'll be here."

Officer Goff frowned a little. "I know being shut up in this place has to be getting old already. Is there anything I can do to make things better?"

"No, I'm fine. I thought I'd watch the ball game when it starts."

"Well, let me know if you think of anything you need. Otherwise, I'm going to take a look around, and then I'll be out in my car. You have my number."

Aubrey closed the door before she gave up all pretense of trying to smile. This couldn't go on forever. The walls were already closing in on her. She could only get lost in a book or a movie for so long before she started pacing the floors. Jonah called a couple of times a day on the burner phone he'd gotten for her. Those calls were her one real lifeline to the outside world. They talked for a half an hour or more about everything but her case for most of that time. Then, right at the end, he'd given her a very brief summary of what was going on. It wasn't that he was simply being succinct; it was more that there was nothing new to report.

Resigning herself to another boring evening, she turned on the television for background noise and settled in to read. At least she had dinner to look forward to.

Aubrey finished the final page in the romance she'd been reading with a smile on her face. The story had held her attention right up until the happy ending. She got up and stretched to ease the huge number of kinks she had in her back and neck from sitting on the lumpy couch.

Dinner was due to arrive soon. Maybe Officer Goff would like to eat in the kitchen with her instead of juggling her food out in her car. Just in case, she would set the table for two. No sooner had she put out two plates and some mismatched flatware than the doorbell rang. Perfect timing. She hustled to the front door, looking forward to having a real human to talk to even for just a minute.

But it wasn't Officer Goff standing there. No, it was Jonah holding out a huge paper bag from a nearby restaurant. He was wearing a T-shirt and matching baseball cap that had the restaurant's logo on them. "Your order, ma'am."

She grinned at him. "Wow, that bag looks really heavy. Maybe you could carry it into the kitchen for me."

He winked at her as he came inside. "I live to serve."

After locking the door, she followed him into the

kitchen. "So, is delivering meals your new side gig? Does it pay well?"

"Considering I only have one customer and paid for the food myself, I'd have to say no." He set the bag on the table. "On the other hand, it meant that I could check on you."

It didn't take long to figure out why he was being so careful. "So you can't stay long."

"No, not if I want this cover to hold up." He glanced down at his shirt. "Although I have to admit I totally rock this look."

Cute, but he wasn't wrong about that since the shirt was the exact shade of blue as his eyes. Regardless, her pulse picked up speed as she realized what he was really saying. "You think he's watching you?"

"There's no way to know for sure."

"So still no progress on the case?"

"We've eliminated one possibility for sure. Ruben was definitely at work when your house was spray-painted. Ross says he was at an AA meeting, but we're waiting for confirmation on that. They're pretty protective of their members' privacy, so I'm not sure if they will actually tell us. Mr. Pyne was at a doctor appointment."

It still bothered her that he seemed so focused on people she counted as friends, or at least used to. "You actually suspected it could be one of them?"

He shrugged. "Not particularly, but we have to consider all possibilities. This guy seems to know a lot about you—where you live, where you work, and even your schedule. I also checked up on your principal. According to the school secretary, he was supposedly at a meeting at the district office. I have someone heading over there in the morning to verify he was there."

She turned her back to him, not wanting him to see the tears in her eyes. "I don't like having my friends and co-workers coming under suspicion. Besides, how can I look them in the face after they learn you've been poking around in their business?"

"If they really are friends, they'll understand that your safety is more important than a few bruised feelings."

His hands settled on her shoulders, and he gently turned her around to face him. "Don't cry, Aubrey. We'll get through this."

Once again, she found herself ignoring the boundaries they'd promised to observe. She stepped into his arms and rested her head against his chest right over the steady beat of his heart as she tried to fight off the tears. He didn't protest. Instead, he kept his hold on her light, letting her draw comfort from his embrace. She finally forced herself to step back. "Sorry about that. You should probably get going. I'm sure you have better things to do than listen to me whine."

He tilted her chin up and looked directly into her eyes. "All things considered, you've handled all of this really well."

"Only because of you. Detective Swahn would have done his best, too, but I doubt he would have hugged me whenever I'm on the verge of falling apart."

Jonah laughed just as she'd hoped he would. "His wife might not appreciate him hugging random women."

"Or kissing them."

The words slipped out before she could stop them. "Sorry, I know we decided we weren't going to go there again."

He sighed and rested his forehead against hers. "No

apologies necessary. The same thought crossed my mind, too. I'd better go before I…before we…"

Jonah took a firm step back. "Look, I really do need to go. I probably shouldn't have come in the first place, but I needed to see for myself that you were all right. For now, Officer Goff is still on duty. I'm not sure who is on after that. If you need anything, hear anything, call them and then me."

"I will."

She trailed after him so she could lock up after he left. Well, that and to spend every second in his company that she could.

Jonah made it halfway across the living room and then spun back toward her with no warning. Before she could ask what was wrong, he enfolded her in his arms and kissed her like there was no tomorrow. The kiss didn't last long, but it packed quite a punch. When he set her back down, he grinned. "No way I'm apologizing for that one."

She liked that he was as breathless as she was. "I wouldn't even think of asking you to."

Jonah walked backward to the door. "Lock up and then go eat your dinner while it's still hot."

She offered him a mocking salute. "Yes, sir. Will do, sir."

He looked back one last time. "Stay safe, Aubrey."

"I'll do my best."

But they both knew no matter how careful she was and no matter how hard he worked, it might not be enough.

FOURTEEN

George set a cup of coffee and an apple fritter down in front of Jonah. "We've barely been working half an hour this morning and already you're frowning big-time. What's wrong?"

Jonah glanced up from the report he'd been reading from one of the private investigators Aubrey had hired. "Mostly frustration. It's like trying to catch a ghost. Even when I find something that might mean something, half the information is redacted."

"What are you looking at?

"One of the reports Aubrey gave us." He put a checkmark by the passage and slid the file across the table to George. "This guy did some checking into an incident that happened at a liberal arts college down in Oregon fifteen years ago. I have no idea how this PI even found out about it, but the case involved two girls being taken at the same time. He eventually decided the differences outweighed the similarities, mostly because it was part of a fraternity rush prank."

Jonah flipped to the second page. "Evidently each pledge had to 'kidnap' two girls and bring them to a party at the frat house. Most of them asked girls they knew, who came along willingly. But this one nitwit took the 'kidnapping' part seriously and grabbed two random girls right on there on campus and took off. Their friends saw what happened and called the campus cops. The local police caught up with them a few minutes later. The kid was only seventeen, and eventually the decision was made to let him off with a warning."

George read through the report next. "Might be worth making a call to the investigating patrol officer if he's still around. There's a good chance he might not remember the case, especially since it didn't end in an arrest or anything."

At this point, Jonah was ready to follow any breadcrumb. "I'll make the call."

Lunchtime had come and gone without any response to his inquiry into the case down in Oregon. The detective had been out of the office when Jonah had called. Waiting was never his strong suit, and it didn't help that they were running into nothing but dead ends.

He'd just finished reading through the last of the private investigator's reports when his phone finally rang. "Detective Kelly."

"This is Detective Jouvin. I hear you're looking for me."

"Yeah, I'm working on a cold case that's heated up. Twelve years ago two young women were kidnapped. One was never heard from again, but the second was set free. Now it looks like the same guy is coming after her again. I have questions about a case you handled fifteen years ago. It's a long shot, but we're doing our best to run down every possibility."

"Which one?"

Jonah gave him a quick summary of the investigator's report. "Sorry that I don't have more specifics. It sounds like no formal charges were filed, maybe because the kid was underage even though he was in college. I don't know how the investigator even found out about it. I tried calling him, too, but his phone is out of service, and his website is gone. I haven't had a chance to see if something happened to him or if he retired and moved. You were my next best chance to find out more about the kid."

"Give me a second to think about it."

Finally, the other detective spoke again. "I remember the case. I can't tell you much because the case never went anywhere. As I recall, the college handled it internally. As far as I know, the kid was let off with a warning, no formal prosecution of any kind. I was only a patrol officer at the time, so it wasn't my call to make. I figured his age was one factor since he was just shy of eighteen."

He sighed. "I assumed the fact that his parents had a ton of money and friends in the right places made the real difference. The college ended up accepting the kid's story that he'd misunderstood what the fraternity brothers wanted him to do. The parents pulled him out of the school right afterward and transferred him to a different college up your way."

What else could he ask that the detective would be able to answer? "And did the kid manage to convince you he was telling the truth about it just being a misunderstanding?"

Jouvin didn't immediately respond. Finally, he said, "Off the record, let's just say the kid was clocked going thirty miles an hour over the speed limit in the opposite direction of the frat house."

"Thanks, Detective Jouvin. You've been a lot of help."

"Whether he is your guy or not, I hope you find the guy you're hunting."

"Me, too."

As soon as Jonah hung up, he grabbed the file and his notes and headed for Captain Martine's office. They needed to reach out to the college in Oregon to see if they could learn anything else—like that kid's name.

Aubrey stared out into the backyard of the safe house. Since the sun had already set, there wasn't much to see. At the best of times, the view didn't have much to recommend it—grass dotted with dandelions, weed-infested flower beds, and several half-dead bushes. It was a sad state of affairs that the run-down mess was the most interesting thing she'd seen all day.

Sighing, she lowered the blinds and returned to the living room. She'd finished her last book earlier, and it would be tomorrow before anyone could bring her more. At least there was a movie on soon that would break up the monotony. It was one of her favorite space operas with great special effects and enough romance to make things interesting.

The question was what to do until then. It was a little too early for dinner, not that she was excited about tonight's menu. One frozen dinner tasted pretty much like another.

Still too restless to relax, she moved the coffee table closer to the couch and the two upholstered chairs out of the way to make enough room to go through her yoga routine. After that warmed up her muscles, she'd do the routine her self-defense instructor had taught her. She'd started taking classes not long after she'd been released. Not only did the two disciplines keep her physically fit, they gave her a sense of empowerment and some hope she'd be able to protect herself in the future.

She'd barely gotten started when a strange noise from out front caught her attention. A weird popping sound was immediately followed by the sound of breaking glass. By that point, Aubrey's heart was pounding so hard she couldn't hear anything at all. That didn't stop her from crawling the few feet to the coffee table to where she'd left the phone. She called her guard's number and held her breath as it started to ring. When someone answered, it wasn't Officer Goff.

"Well, hello, Aubrey. It's been a while since we last talked. I'm guessing you didn't miss me, but I suppose that is only understandable."

She was pretty sure it was a male voice, but the mechanical distortion made it impossible to know much more than that. "Where's Officer Goff?"

"She's bleeding all over her car, but she's still breathing. Tell her you're alive, Officer."

There was a soft moan. "Aubrey, call 911. Don't open the—"

"Do that, and your cop friend is dead for sure. Come along peacefully, and she might survive until someone finds her. Either way, you'll still end up leaving with me. It's your choice. Do you really want to be responsible for her death?"

No matter what he said, Aubrey wouldn't really be the one who killed Officer Goff. There was also no guarantee that the kidnapper wouldn't kill her even if Aubrey did cooperate. Regardless, there was only one option that she could live with. Aubrey closed her eyes and prayed hard for Officer Goff's safety. *Please, Father, hold her in Your hands until help can arrive.*

At the same time, Aubrey dialed 911 and whispered her name and begged them to send help quickly because Officer Goff had been shot. And finally she asked the operator to tell Detective Kelly that none of this was his fault. He wouldn't believe that, and she hated knowing her disappearance would cause him more pain. He was already living with the guilt of his friend's death, and she didn't want him to shoulder the blame for whatever happened to her. Aware that time was running out for Officer Goff, she shoved the phone out of sight under the sofa in case the man came inside. There was no telling what he'd do to her or Officer Goff if he checked her call history and learned that she'd defied his order not to call the authorities.

Then she pushed herself up to her feet and unlocked the door.

Jonah had the responding officer on speakerphone as he drove like a madman toward the safe house. He'd been on his way to pick up dinner when the call about Aubrey had come in. "How long has Ms. Sims been gone?"

"Near as we can figure, forty minutes tops. Her call came in less than half an hour ago. We arrived on scene less than ten minutes after that."

"How is Officer Goff doing?"

"In pain, but alert. She refused to let them transport her to the hospital until she speaks to you. The EMTs aren't happy."

That was understandable, but he was grateful he'd get to talk to her before the ambulance whisked her away. If she needed surgery, it could be hours or maybe even tomorrow before he'd have a chance to talk to her again. "I'm almost there."

"I'll tell them."

Jonah swerved in and out of traffic with his lights flashing for the last few blocks to the safe house. Once there, he'd talk to Officer Goff first and then check out the scene to see what he could learn. If the kidnapper was as careful as he had been so far, Jonah wasn't expecting to find much. The only good news was that the nature of Officer Goff's injury wasn't life-threatening. She'd taken a bullet to the shoulder and some minor cuts from broken glass.

He reminded himself to be grateful and give thanks for that much. Hopefully, she'd be able to give them something to go on, preferably a description of her attacker or a license plate. They'd need every possible detail they could get in order to start tracking Aubrey's whereabouts. It killed him that even now she was reliving her worst nightmares. He railed against the injustice of it all. Aubrey had to be scared out of her wits, and yet she'd asked dispatch to tell him that none of this was his fault.

Yeah, he got what she meant. It was her kidnapper who had set all of this in motion. Her intentions were good, but the truth was that once again Jonah had failed to protect someone who had depended on him. He wasn't sure how he'd survive if he failed to bring Aubrey home safely. If he lost her, he wasn't sure he would even want to. That was an awful realization, but that was where his head was right now. The truth was that somehow she'd become the center of his universe in the short time he'd known her. If he didn't trust his own ability to find her, then he needed to put his trust in a higher power. *Father, I know You brought Aubrey into my life for a reason. Please watch over her until I can find her.*

A new sense of calm washed over him, letting him think

clearly for the first time since the call had come in. He turned down the street where the safe house was located but had to park two blocks away. The responding officers had blocked off traffic up ahead, and the emergency vehicles took up most of the road. He locked his vehicle and took off at a slow lope.

It was tempting to rush inside the safe house and look around, but he owed it to Officer Goff to check on her first. He flashed his badge at each cop he passed and kept walking. He wasn't surprised at the number of officers swarming around the crime scene. One of their own had been shot, and a person under their protection had been taken. No one would rest until the culprit was found and brought to justice.

It was another reminder that Jonah wasn't alone in this.

A few seconds later, he approached the EMTs who were riding herd on Officer Goff. Jonah nodded at them and waited for their permission to approach their patient. "Make it quick, Detective. She's hurting and might need a transfusion."

"Will do."

He moved up to stand next to the gurney. "Officer Goff, what can you tell me?"

She looked like roadkill, her eyes dull with pain. That didn't stop her from trying to sit up to make her report even though she couldn't stifle a whimper when she moved. The EMT started forward, but Jonah waved him off. "Easy does it, April. Lie back and relax. You don't want to make the bleeding worse. I'm right here. Tell me what happened so these folks can get you the care you need."

Latching on to his arm, she tugged him down closer and spoke in fits and starts. "No idea where the guy came from…appeared out of nowhere and shot through the window. Best guess…he used a silencer since no neighbors came running out…must have parked on a side street. I did see a big sedan…older model, silver or gray…pull out of the street behind me a few minutes later. No way to know if it was him…it turned the other direction, so it didn't pass by me."

"Can you give me any kind of description of him?"

She started to nod, but winced again as if even the smallest movement hurt. "Tall. Maybe six feet, six-one. Wore all black, including a ski mask. Used something to distort his voice. Definitely male, though. Looked fit. Swimmer's build, not a body builder. He cuffed my hands to the steering wheel so I couldn't call it in. Aubrey must have heard something, because she called me. He grabbed the phone and answered. She asked if I was okay. He held the phone so I could speak. Tried to tell her to call it in. He threatened to kill me if she did. She called anyway."

Tears trickled down her face. "She's a brave woman. She let him take her to keep him from killing me." Her eyes glittered with tears. "I'm so sorry he got her, sir."

"We are all." Jonah patted her gently on her uninjured arm. "It's time you head to the hospital. I'll take over from here. You concentrate on getting better."

She let her eyes drift closed. "Get her back."

"I will do my best."

And pray that his best was good enough.

It didn't take long for Jonah to walk through the safe house. There was no sign of violence. That was the good news. The bad news was that he suspected it was true that Aubrey had surrendered to her abductor hoping to save Officer Goff's life. He would've done the same thing. That didn't mean he was happy that she'd made that decision. She had known help was on the way. If she'd stayed barricaded inside the house, she might've been able to hold out until the officers responded. They'd arrived on scene only minutes after she'd made the call.

But there was no way she could have known how fast they would get there. If the kidnapper had made a determined effort, he could have broken in through a window or even kicked in the door. Disobeying his orders would have only increased the likelihood that he would have executed Officer Goff in retaliation. Who knew what he would have done to Aubrey herself?

The front door opened. He looked to see who had arrived and wasn't surprised to see it was Captain Martine. "What's our status?"

"Officer Goff took a bullet in the shoulder. She insisted on staying here until she talked to me. If the wound was life-threatening, the EMTs would have taken her to the hospital right away."

"At least there's that much good news." Captain Martine looked around the living room before continuing. "My next stop is to speak with her parents. After that, I'll be at the hospital."

Jonah was relieved he wasn't going to have to face them, but he felt compelled to offer. "If you'd rather I talked to Mr. and Mrs. Sims…"

His captain shook his head. "No, I want you focused on the case. Keep me posted."

"I will."

A second later, his phone rang. A glance at the screen

told him it was George Swahn. The older man had remained at headquarters, figuring he'd do more good there.

"What's up?"

"I think we may have something. That detective you talked to from Oregon called again. How soon will you be finished up at there?"

Jonah looked around. The techs were still processing the scene. Other officers were working their way through the neighborhood canvasing the area for witnesses. Deciding there wasn't much he could contribute to the effort, he started for the door. "I'm on my way."

FIFTEEN

Aubrey heard a soft moan. With considerable effort, she pried open one eye and looked around to see who had made the noise. The glaring sunlight shining in through the window across the room set off a firestorm of pain inside her head. Relieved to find no one in sight, she let her eyelid drop back down again and slept. She had no idea how much time had passed when another whimper woke her up again. At least this time, she immediately understood that she was the one making the noise.

Considering how bad she felt at that moment, she wasn't surprised. When she tried to lift her head to look around, a wave of dizziness left her queasy and shaking. The darkness still lapping at the edges of her mind proved stronger than her ability to resist it, and she slid back into unconsciousness again.

By the time she finally woke up completely, the sunlight coming through the one window in the room had dimmed considerably. That was one good bit of news. The other was that she was still alone. On the downside, apparently a whole lot of hours had passed since she'd been abducted. She wouldn't be left here alone for long.

Wherever *here* was.

How had she even gotten there? The last clear memory she had was of opening the front door of the safe house. A man dressed all in black had blindfolded her and then dragged her down the street and around the corner. There'd been the sound of a trunk lid opening right before he'd picked her up and dropped her inside. A second later, he'd stabbed her with something sharp. That was the last thing she remembered. She could only guess he'd shot her full of some knockout drug. Considering how long she'd been out, whatever had been in the syringe had packed quite a punch. Either that, or he'd given her another dose at some point.

Her brain was starting to fire on more cylinders, but there were still a lot of gaps in her memory that needed to be filled in. But before she could do that, she had more pressing matters to take care of. Moving slowly, she pushed herself up into a sitting position. When her head quit spinning, she took a slow look around. It took only a second to recognize her surroundings, because she'd been there before. From what she could tell, the small cabin hadn't changed at all over the past twelve years.

Her pulse picked up speed, which didn't help her headache. On the other hand, maybe having her blood rush through her veins faster than normal would help clear the drug out of her system. She started to swing her legs over the side of the bed, but it didn't go as planned. Her left one moved easily enough, but her right leg was weighed down with something. She tried again, only to realize the problem was the heavy metal shackle wrapped around her ankle.

It brought back another flash of memory from twelve years ago, one that had haunted her dreams all too often. Just like this time, she'd regained consciousness to find herself and her best friend chained to a metal ring sticking up out of the concrete floor. They'd desperately tried without success to break free of their chains. They'd also pounded on the walls and screamed themselves hoarse hoping that someone would hear them.

All their efforts had garnered them was bruised hands and sore throats. That wasn't going to stop her from trying again. She managed to swing both of her legs over the edge of the bed and scooted forward to plant her feet flat on the floor. Proud of her progress, she took a deep breath and tried to stand. After two more attempts to stay upright, she shuffled toward the curtain that served as the bathroom door. The facilities were as primitive as they were last time, but she used them anyway.

With that taken care of, she decided to check out the cooler and paper bag sitting next to the cabin door. Whoever the guy was who'd dragged her back here, he was a creature of habit. Just like before, the bag contained apples, potato chips and a variety of individual snacks. The cooler had a layer of ice on the bottom. Nestled into the melting mess were a dozen bottles of water and soft drinks. There was also a plastic container filled with prepackaged sandwiches, the kind that could be bought at any gas station.

Was it safe to drink the water or eat the food? The bottom line was that she had no choice. In order to face off against her captor, she'd need every ounce of strength she could muster. With grim determination, she picked a bottle of water at random and studied it for signs that it had been tampered with. The seal was unbroken, and there was no damage to the plastic or the label. The last time the food had also been safe to eat. Maybe he didn't want to risk having his captives overdose and spoil his fun.

She instantly slammed the door on that line of thinking. Right now, her focus needed to be on escaping. It was imperative to find some way out of this nightmare before he came back. Because he would return. And this time there wouldn't be any coin flipping to offer her a last-minute reprieve. She twisted the lid off the bottle and took a big drink. Grabbing an apple and a pack of peanut butter crackers, she shuffled back over to the bed and sat down.

Already, she was feeling better. The fuzziness in her head was all but gone, and her stomach had settled down. What next?

She tugged on the chain, knowing full well what to expect. It was just long enough to allow her to reach every corner of the one-room cabin, but no farther. Even if she could somehow open the door, she wouldn't be able to step outside. The same was true if she found a way to remove the bars on the only window. After glancing outside, she paced the width of the cabin half a dozen times to stretch her legs before returning to the window.

The view was nothing but huge cedars and Douglas firs for as far as she could see. She suspected that the cabin was tucked away at the far end of a dirt road somewhere in the Cascade Mountains. From what she'd seen outside the window, the road came to a stop right in front of the cabin, so no chance of a helpful stranger driving by. Instead, eventually she'd hear a car approach, and there was only one person who would be coming. She drew some strength from knowing that she'd finally learn the identity of the man who had altered the direction of her entire life.

As she stood there, she realized she was shivering. Some of it was due to her increasing fear, but it was also likely the temperature was dropping now that the sun had set.

She picked out another snack and retreated to sit on the bed. The blanket was thin and worn, but it was better than nothing. After wrapping it around her shoulders, Aubrey ate a granola bar and some string cheese while she contemplated her situation.

Even if hope was in limited supply right now, there was one major difference between what happened twelve years ago and now. This time someone was out there looking for her who knew exactly what had happened. Jonah might not know who had taken her, but he wouldn't stop looking until he found the answer. Regardless of how this ended, he would also do his best to make sure her parents got closure.

She could only imagine what they were going through right now. After all, they already knew what it was like to have their only child go missing. The fact that they'd been lucky enough to get Aubrey back didn't mean they'd ever forgotten that pain—or the fear that it could happen again. She hated knowing the terror they were living with right now. Worse yet, they'd want someone to blame, and she was sure they would aim all of their anger right at Jonah. She didn't want any of them to shoulder the blame for this. They weren't the ones who shot Officer Goff or dragged Aubrey back to this cabin.

She wished she could tell them that herself. Instead, Aubrey did the only thing she could do. She prayed. *Father, I ask You for the strength to face whatever comes. Not just for me, but for my parents, my friends, and most of all, for Jonah and his coworkers. Give them comfort, and let them feel Your healing spirit. My one regret is that I didn't tell Jonah how much he means to me. He's a good man, and I hope he finds peace in Your love. Amen.*

Her energy at low ebb, she curled up on the bed and drifted off to sleep. She'd need to be rested when that car came driving up the road.

Jonah had been up all night, and it was looking as if sleep was on hold for the foreseeable future. George had indeed found a string, and they'd tugged on it as hard as possible without getting anywhere. As it turned out, while Jonah was at the safe house Detective Jouvin had called back. He'd unearthed one more tidbit of information when he'd found his spiral notebook from back then. He didn't know why, but the kid had registered at the college using his middle name and his mother's maiden name. Evidently, his legal name was actually her last name and his father's, separated with a hyphen. Anyway, Jouvin's notes had listed the kid as L. Mark Dennison.

It wasn't much, and they didn't find anyone with that name in any of the searches they'd tried. For most of the night, they'd watched traffic camera footage looking for a car that met Officer Goff's vague description. The captain had finally ordered George to go home and sleep. He'd made the same suggestion to Jonah, but didn't get far.

Meanwhile, Sergeant Decker had been keeping Jonah supplied with coffee and food while he worked. Finally, he'd pulled up a chair and sat down. After studying their notes on the white board on the wall, he said, "Tell me what you've got so far."

When Jonah shot him a dark look, Decker didn't blink. "Talking it out helps sometimes, so it's worth a try. You've looked at all this stuff until you're not really seeing it anymore. Tell me what you're thinking. I know about what happened twelve years ago. Start with what's happened recently"

Fine. For sure, he wasn't making any progress on his own. Jonah got up and walked around to stand in front of the white board. "Aubrey Sims said she'd been feeling as if someone has been watching her. The note was sent to her private mailbox, and flowers were delivered to her house. That means that guy has been watching her for some time. He also knows where she works, because that's where her tire was spiked. That's when I convinced her to take a leave of absence."

Decker looked surprised. "She told them that she had a stalker?"

Jonah shook his head. "No, she let them think that she had a personal problem that needed her immediate attention."

"Good thinking."

"I followed her home from school and made sure she got inside safely. Right after that, she discovered a message had been painted on her bedroom window. The captain made the decision to move her to a safe house, but the guy we're looking for found her there. He could have followed me or one of the other officers."

"Suspects?"

Pointing to that particular list, Jonah pointed at the top name. "Ross Easton was the fiancé of the girl who never made it home last time. Evidently, he used to stalk Aubrey, but he claims he stopped that nonsense when he got sober. For what it's worth, I believe him. Evidently he wasn't very good at stalking, because she would see him hanging around. She confirmed she hadn't seen or talked to Ross in years."

"Next up is Ruben Jacobs, the evening custodian at her school. That would explain how he knows where she works. Not sure if Ruben would have access to her records to get her address or PO box number. We verified he was at work when the window was painted. He's also in his early sixties, so he doesn't exactly fit the profile. He's pretty low on my list of suspects."

Jonah pointed at the next name. "Riley Pyne is the father of the girl who didn't make it home twelve years ago. He and his wife used to make Aubrey's life pretty miserable, but Mr. Pyne's health isn't good. I can't see him pulling off an abduction of a healthy young woman, at least not alone."

That left just one name on the list. "This guy's name is up here mainly because there's something about him I don't like. He's the principal at Aubrey's school. She's known him for a couple of years, ever since he took the job. By all reports, the guy is well liked and respected. However, we haven't been able to confirm for sure where he was at a couple of crucial times over the past week. That said, it's coming up on the end of the school year. Evidently that means he's in and out of the building for meetings at the district office."

"Is he single?"

"Yeah. Why?"

Decker hesitated but finally said, "Could that be why you don't like him? Because he could be interested in Ms. Sims on a personal level?"

Jonah growled, "What does that have to do with anything?"

"Lie to me if you want to, Detective, but don't lie to yourself. If your gut is telling you there's something off about this guy, fine. But make sure that's why he's at the top of your list."

The sergeant was right to question Jonah's motivations even if it made him want to toss the man out of the conference room. He closed his eyes and thought about everything he knew about Aubrey's boss and then summarized it. "Principal Peale was born and raised right outside of Seattle. He graduated from college with a degree in elementary education and a master's in school administration or some such thing. After that, he taught school in Florida for five years before moving back to Washington State. He's divorced, no kids."

"All of that sounds pretty normal. So what is it about him that bothers you?"

"Like I said, the kidnapper has been observing Aubrey for a while now. That would be pretty easy to do if he actually worked with her. As principal, he'd have access to her personnel file. On Aubrey's second to last day at school, she worked late. She was walking out to the parking lot where I was going to meet her and follow her home. The janitor offered to walk her out since everyone else was already gone. She suggested Ruben watch her from the door instead. Either way, Aubrey wasn't technically alone. That's when she found out her tire had been spiked. That's the same thing the kidnapper did twelve years ago."

He stopped to sip his coffee and review the next details in his head to make sure he had the order right. "Her principal just happened to come back to the school right when she spotted the spike in her tire. Something about picking up some papers for a meeting the next morning. Again, that could be true. I can tell you this much for certain— he definitely didn't like me being the one who changed the tire for Aubrey. I wanted to bring it in to the forensics lab, but I wasn't about to tell him that. He kept suggesting that she call for her emergency road service to come deal with the tire instead."

"Did he know who you were or what you do?"

He had to give that some thought. "She said I was a friend, but I'm pretty sure she introduced me as Detective Jonah Kelly."

"If Peale is your guy, knowing she has a cop hanging around had to give him pause even if you really were simply her friend. He'd have to wonder if you were actually there in your professional capacity. After all, why would she need someone to follow her home? Is there more?"

"Yeah, there is. He also wasn't at the school when the spray painting happened. One of the patrol officers checked with the district office to see if he was there. There had been a meeting, but it apparently ended early. The person the officer spoke to said she wasn't sure when he left the administration building. The trouble is that there are several exits. A couple of people remember talking to him after the meeting, though. Still, depending on when he actually left, there's a good chance he could've made it to Aubrey's and back to school without anyone noticing if he went missing for a while."

Decker nodded in approval. "Okay, so it's a lot of little things that may or may not add up to something significant."

"That's the problem. We've got nothing solid to go on. In the meantime, whoever the guy is, he has Aubrey."

Which made him physically ill.

Decker pointed to the other side of the board. "You

haven't mentioned anyone by that name. Who is L. Mark Dennison?"

Jonah launched into a brief description of the private investigator's report and the small amount of information they'd gotten from Detective Jouvin. "We did some searching under that name and didn't find anything. Either he's not in the area or else he's changed his name again."

"Do you know what the *L* stands for?"

No, but come to think of it, he did know one person whose name started with that letter. How could he have not seen that before now?

Decker leaned forward, elbows on the table. "You've spotted something."

Jonah pointed at the *L* and smiled. "Principal Peale's first name is Lyle."

SIXTEEN

The waiting was the worst. A second night had come and gone with no sign of her captor. Not that Aubrey wanted him to return, but what if he never came back? He'd left her only a minimal amount of water and food, with no indication of how long it was supposed to last her. What happened if she ran out? Would she survive long enough for someone else to find her? So many scary questions with no answers. It wasn't the first time that panic had threatened to overwhelm her. Rather than give in to it, she'd turned to her faith and the firm belief that God would never abandon her.

Remembering that gave Aubrey the strength to make plans. To take control of the few things she could, starting with rationing her supplies. Half of a stale sandwich washed down with a few sips of water hadn't been a very satisfying breakfast, but for now it was better to err on the side of caution.

She admired the view from the window. While there wasn't much for her to be grateful for at the moment, the incredible beauty of nature was soothing. Focusing on a dense forest of enormous cedar trees was so much better for her emotional state than cowering on the bed with nothing to see but bare wooden walls. Finally, she shuffled back to the center of the room and once again went through her yoga stretches, or at least the ones she could do dragging a chain around. Once she warmed up her muscles, she flowed right into her self-defense routine.

Not that her self-defense techniques had helped her avoid being captured, but that was because someone else's life had been hanging in the balance. Going on the attack would've almost certainly ended in Officer Goff's death. That had left Aubrey with no choice but to willingly go with her captor. Jonah might not agree with her decision, but he would've done the same thing. If given the choice to give his life to save his partner's, Jonah wouldn't have hesitated. The man was a hero right down to the bone.

She wanted to tell him that in person, which meant she needed to be ready when she next confronted her captor. The chain clanked as she flowed from one position to the next, moving slower than normal. She'd gotten tangled in the chain earlier when she'd done a spinning move and gone down in an awkward heap. The ill-timed maneuver had resulted in a few new bruises, but no serious injuries. After that, she'd slowed everything down to make sure she was in fighting form when the time came.

As she finished her second round of exercise, a sound outside the cabin caught her attention. Freezing in position, she listened hard, although it was difficult to hear much of anything over her own ragged breathing and racing pulse. A second later, her worst fears were confirmed—a vehicle was headed her way.

She wished she had been able to fashion a weapon of some kind, but there wasn't anything in the cabin other than the cooler and the narrow bed. She'd hoped that she could somehow dismantle the frame, but it turned out to be nothing more than a box made out of plywood. Right now, her best option was to shake up one of the soft drinks as hard as she could. Then, when he walked into the cabin, she could pop the top and spray it in his face. The ploy might work in theory, but she might be better off just heaving the full can at his head.

A minute later, an older-model car parked in front of the cabin, at an angle that made it impossible to see the driver. Aubrey watched and waited for him to get out of the vehicle so she could finally get a look at the man who had plagued her life for so many years. When he finally stepped into sight, her mind couldn't process what she was seeing.

This was no stranger. She knew him well, or at least she'd always thought she did. Her brain struggled to connect the dots. How had her boss happened to stumble across the cabin where she was being held captive? For a single moment, hope surged that Principal Peale would break down the door and whisk her back to civilization. When he spotted her staring out of the window, he smiled and started toward the door carrying a pair of grocery sacks.

Aubrey watched in horror as he walked through the door, his familiar smile firmly in place as he set the grocery bags on the floor. "Good morning, Aubrey. I brought more ice and a few more supplies. Sorry to say that I can't stay long. School isn't out yet, and I have to maintain my usual schedule as much as possible."

"Why are you doing this?"

"I would think the answer to that would be obvious." He pointed toward the bags. "You need fresh food and water. Without proper refrigeration, this stuff won't last long. I'm replenishing your supplies so you don't get sick from eating bad food."

He dumped the new ice into the cooler and then added a few more bottles of water along with some new sandwiches. When he was done, he set a box of saltine crackers and a jar of peanut butter on top of the cooler. "I didn't think to ask. You're not allergic to peanuts, are you?"

She shook her head. "No, but I wasn't asking about the food. I was asking why you brought me here."

His usual friendly smile slid away to be replaced with one that made her skin crawl. "Don't ask questions you really don't want the answers to, Aubrey. Let's just say that we're going to have fun together. At least it will be fun for me. Unfortunately, the good times can't start until after school is out and I'm on summer vacation. I have a few meetings the day after the kids leave for the summer, but then I'll be able to devote all my attention to our time together. Until then, I'll stop by when I can to bring more supplies."

"Why now and why me, Lyle? We've been working together for almost two years."

His creepy smile was back in full force. "Anticipation is part of the game. I've loved knowing that this day would come and that you had no idea. That aside, letting you go twelve years ago always felt like a bit of unfinished business. I've entertained other guests over that time, of course, but somehow you've never been far from my mind."

He checked the time and frowned. "I really need to leave. See you soon."

This time her chills had nothing to do with the cool temperature outside of the cabin. "I will pray the Lord will heal your sickness."

He'd been about to walk out the door, but Lyle charged back across the cabin to grab Aubrey by her hair and gave it a yank. "I'm not sick, Aubrey. You might want to watch how you talk to me. I expect to be treated with respect. That was something your friend Marta learned the hard way. You really, really don't want to see me angry."

Then, just as if a switch had been flipped, he released her and backed away. "Enjoy your time here. I'll be back soon."

As he drove away, she collapsed on the bed and cried.

Jonah had gone home and crashed last night, but he didn't sleep for long. His dreams had turned dark and bloody, filled with gaunt images of Gino and Aubrey hovering just out of his reach with their hands outstretched and begging for his help. Whenever he tried to latch on to their hands, they faded out of sight, only to pop back into view in another direction. Finally realizing that trying to sleep was futile, he'd gotten dressed and driven back to the precinct.

After buying a bag of breakfast sandwiches at the closest drive-through, he'd arrived about two hours before sunrise only to find his boss was already there. Over coffee and egg sandwiches, Captain Martine listened in silence as Jonah reviewed everything they'd learned since the last time they'd spoken. "We've verified that Lyle Peale's full name is Lyle Mark Dennison-Peale. It seems that he's used different combinations of those names over the years. When he left the school in Oregon, he enrolled in his next college as Lyle Peale. We also traced his work history in Florida, where he changed schools almost every year. Not sure why."

He stopped to scan his notes again. "We did a search

for similar cases to ours in the general area where he lived in Florida and found two that line up pretty closely. From what we know now, both cases are currently unsolved with no witnesses and no suspects. Forensics are pretty much nonexistent and victims were never found. I requested copies of the case files, and the investigating detectives promised to have them faxed overnight."

"Sounds promising. One bit of good news is that Officer Goff should be discharged from the hospital tomorrow or the day after. She'll need some physical therapy, but the feeling is there won't be any long-term problems with her shoulder."

Jonah had personal experience with the kind of damage a bullet could do to a major joint, so he was happy to hear her prognosis was so positive. It hit him that he'd missed two physical therapy appointments over the past few days, but too bad. Right now, his knee was the least of his concerns.

The captain's expression turned more serious. "Just so you know, I did speak to Ms. Sims's family personally. To say they're up in arms that we let this happen on our watch is putting it mildly. I assured them that we had an entire team working on finding their daughter. It was all I could do to convince them not to go running to the newspapers or posting anything on social media. I told them those actions could push her captor into rash action. I'm not sure they'll listen to me, but I can't say I really blame them."

"Me neither." Jonah could only imagine how the couple had reacted. "They've been through this before and know full well they had been lucky to get their daughter back. It has to be tearing them up having it happen all over again."

He wasn't telling his boss anything new. When the captain's phone rang, he answered it and asked the other person to hold for a second. "Jonah, just so you know, I've already reached out to the prosecutor's office to apprise him of the situation. Keep me posted of any new findings."

Jonah knew a dismissal when he heard one. "Yes, sir."

He left the captain's office and headed back to the conference room where he and his small team had holed up to work. He spent the next hour reviewing the files that had come in on the two cases from Florida. Even though there was no helpful evidence, the cases were near matches to both the kidnapping twelve years ago and the current one. It was killing him to know that Aubrey was out there somewhere and wondering if anyone would ever find her. "Have we learned anything new?"

Decker lifted his hand to catch Jonah's attention. "The vehicle Peale drives to work is a dark blue SUV, but we've found he also has an older-model sedan registered under Mark Dennison. It's listed as silver and would possibly fit the description of the vehicle Officer Goff saw pull out of the street down the block from the safe house the night of the kidnapping."

Okay, now the pieces were finally starting to fall into place. Each new fact helped convince him that they were on the right track. His greatest fear was that by focusing all of the attention on Aubrey's boss, they might miss something that might point in another direction. If that happened, the mistake could prove fatal to Aubrey. As soon as that thought crossed his mind, he silently prayed that the Lord would continue to guide their footsteps.

At that point, George Swahn joined the discussion. "Once we found out about that vehicle, I went back and screened the traffic cam footage from around the time when Aubrey's tire was spiked at the school. I couldn't find a clear enough angle to get the license plate number, but there was a brief glimpse of a silver sedan of the appropriate vintage turning into a parking lot about an hour before she actually walked out of the building. I couldn't find any footage showing it leaving again. There's no way to know for sure it was Peale's car, but my gut feeling is that it was him. It would make sense if he was going to take the risk of spiking her tire at their place of employment that he wouldn't do it driving his usual vehicle."

Jonah couldn't find fault with the man's logic. "I agree. I can personally testify that he was driving the blue SUV when he showed up later. Maybe he'd left his SUV in the same parking lot and switched back after spiking the tire. It would be worth checking to see what kind of businesses are in that area. We haven't seen the sedan near his condo, and he has to keep it somewhere. Maybe he rents a storage unit near the school."

George grinned. "Good thinking. I'll do some checking."

Jonah moved onto his next question. "Have we had any luck tracing properties listed under any of his names?"

"Not yet, but we're working on it."

"I'm thinking that will be the key to catching him. This guy is too careful not to have some place that he can control completely. He wouldn't want any nosy neighbors close by who might get curious about why he comes and goes at odd times or hear something that would have them calling the police."

Jonah circled around the end of the table to study the map they'd posted on the wall. He pointed to the red push-pins that marked where the school was located and the condo where Peale lived. "Having said all of that, it's got to be close enough to where he lives and works that he can get there and back within a reasonable amount of time. We should restrict the title searches to a fifty-mile radius first. If we can't find anything there, we'll expand the search."

Decker asked, "What are you going to do next?"

Jonah needed to sit down and give his leg a break before it stiffened up completely. After taking his seat, he rubbed his knee, not bothering to try to hide his actions from the others. "I'm going to update the captain again. It's an outside shot with our lack of hard evidence, but maybe we can get a search warrant for his condo and his vehicles, at least the one we can find. If we can find a storage unit, I'll add it to the list. I'll also have patrol drive by Peale's condo again to see if there's any sign of the silver sedan."

Decker had installed a coffeemaker on a low cabinet in the back corner. He got up and brought the pot over to top off Jonah's cup and then did the same for everyone else. As he circled the table, he asked, "What do you think would happen if you paid a visit to Peale at the school? Maybe under the guise of checking to see if they'd had any more problems with vandalism since Ms. Sims's tire was damaged."

Jonah considered the idea, but it didn't feel right. "I'll think about it. I'm concerned that approaching him for any reason right now would only panic him. We know he's at work today, which hopefully means we still have a little time before he gets serious about his plans for Aubrey. I think he might have taken her this week because he knew his schedule would be erratic. Because he has meetings and other stuff going on, it makes it more difficult for people to notice if he disappears for short periods of time."

George looked up from whatever he'd been reading. "Grabbing her early was smart thinking. If news of her disappearance came out, he's been doing a good job of making it look like it's been business as usual for him at work."

The coffee was the consistency of tar, but right now Jonah needed that strong jolt of caffeine. "Yeah, the real problem comes when the summer break actually starts in a few days. Once that happens, he'll be free to disappear without anyone noticing. For now, we still have time to find her."

He hoped, because failure wasn't an option.

Jonah needed to get out of the office and do something active. Everyone was working as hard as they could, but they hadn't made any more progress. He picked up his jacket and slipped it on. "I'm going to go by the hospital to see Officer Goff. I have a picture of the type of sedan that Peale owns. I want to see if it looks like the one she saw leaving the area. Then I'm going to swing by to check in on the officer watching the school. On the way back, I'll pick up another round of sandwiches. Any preferences?"

Once he'd written down their orders, he left the building. Before getting into his car, he stopped to enjoy several breaths of cool, fresh air. As soon as he did, a new wave of guilt hit him hard. How could he enjoy anything at all knowing Aubrey was still being held captive? Depending on where Peale had her stashed, she could be cold, hungry, or even in pain. Not to mention scared out of her wits.

He got into the car and rested his forehead on the steering wheel as he fought to regain control of his emotions. He hated this for her, but she was an amazingly strong woman in so many ways. Resilient, too. Yes, her previous captivity had left its mark on her, but Aubrey had still managed to build a good life for herself. She'd done it once, and she'd do it again with God's help—and Jonah's, too, if she'd let him.

For now, he would go visit Officer Goff and then dive back into the investigation. As hard as everyone was working, something had to break on the case soon. *Please, God, let that be true.*

SEVENTEEN

Aubrey bit back a cry of pain. She'd broken another nail, this one badly enough to bleed a little. Shaking her hand, she waited for the initial sting to dissipate and got right back to work. Lyle wouldn't be happy if he saw the damage she'd done to his cooler. Soon after he'd left, she given herself a stern lecture. Lying around and crying wouldn't accomplish anything. Rather than wallow in self-pity, she needed to be proactive and find some way to defend herself. With that in mind, she set about trying to fashion a rudimentary weapon out of the hardware on the cooler.

The collapsible handle was plastic, and probably wouldn't be much good as a weapon. And if she damaged the cooler getting it off, Lyle was bound to notice. That left the wheels. Actually, not the wheels themselves, but the axle that connected them. She was pretty sure it was a metal rod. If she succeeded in removing it, she could prop the wheels back in place, and turn that end against the wall where any damage might not be so obvious.

At the very least, she could use the rod to jab at Lyle's exposed flesh like his face and hands. If she could hurt him badly enough, she might buy herself enough time to make a run for it. Well, if she could manage to get the keys to unlock her shackle first. Her real hope was that she could sharpen one end of the rod enough to pick the lock herself. Lyle wouldn't expect her to be free of her chain, which would buy her another second or two to surprise him.

On her third attempt, the first wheel finally popped off. She tipped the cooler up enough to tug on the other wheel, slowly working it and the metal rod to which it was attached free from the cooler. It took a little more time to remove the second wheel from the axle, leaving her with a steel rod about twelve inches long. Short enough to hide, long enough to do some serious damage. She whipped it through the air and smiled. She wasn't a violent person by nature, but that didn't mean she wasn't going to defend herself.

She'd unloaded most of the food from the cooler to make it easier to maneuver and needed to put it all back. First, though, she turned the cooler around so the side with the wheels would be against the wall. That done, she propped the wheels back in position and collapsed the handle back down. After setting aside a sandwich and a soft drink, she returned the rest of the food to the cooler and latched the lid.

After taking a seat on the bed, she studied the cooler and decided that it was the best she could do under the circumstances. Either it would pass muster, or it wouldn't. Besides, if Lyle stopped to check it out, it might give her an opportunity to go on the attack. Next, she studied the shackle on her ankle. Unfortunately, it was all too obvious the metal rod was too thick to pick the lock. The only way she was going to get free of her chain was to get the keys from Lyle.

She washed down the last bite of stale sandwich with her diet cola and tossed the can into the corner with the rest of the trash she'd accumulated in the time she'd been there. The pile was a sad reminder of how much time had passed since she'd been taken captive. Every minute that ticked by made it that much sooner that Lyle would come back.

Her mother and father had to be going crazy by now. She really hoped that they didn't blame Jonah or the rest of the police for her predicament. Chances were that they would, though. They were a clearer target than the faceless bogeyman from twelve years ago. It made her heart ache knowing the pain they were in when there was nothing she could do to ease it.

No, that wasn't true. She walked over to the window where she closed her eyes and lifted her face to feel the warmth of the sun filtering down through the trees. "Holy Father, grant Your healing peace to my parents and those others who are hurting right now. Remind them of Your love and keep them safe. Amen."

Feeling better, she returned to the bed and stretched out with her new weapon tucked out of sight but close at hand. As she waited for sleep to overtake her, she let her mind drift back to her last happy memory—the moment Jonah had kissed her. For those precious few seconds, she hadn't been the victim of a crime that he had to solve. No, they'd been a man and a woman connecting in a whole different way. She'd felt cherished, loved, normal.

She hoped she lived long enough to feel that way again.

Jonah had sent the patrol officer watching the school off to grab some lunch and stretch his legs a bit. While he waited for his return, Jonah decided to check in with his team. They put him on speakerphone so he wouldn't have to repeat himself. "First, Officer Goff is doing great. She'll go home tomorrow. The docs say she'll have to be on light duty for a few weeks before she's cleared to return to patrol. She also says while she can't say for sure, she thinks the picture I showed her looks a lot like the car she saw. Now we just need to find it."

Decker spoke next. "There is a storage space place on that stretch of road near the school. Haven't verified if he has a spot there, though."

Even without verification, Jonah was sure another piece had just fallen into place. "Anything else?"

A knock on his window startled him. He looked up to see Lyle Peale staring down at him. "Gotta go, guys. We'll talk again soon."

He rolled the window down. "Can I help you?"

Lyle tilted his head to the side as if studying an interesting bug. "A parent who lives down the street called the school to let us know that someone has been parked here all morning, just sitting in the car. I thought I'd come out and check before I called the police."

His smile turned a bit feral. "But didn't Aubrey say you were a detective? If so, I guess the police are already here. Care to tell me why you're hanging around an elementary school? Because if there is a threat of some kind to our students, I should know about it."

"Nope, no threat. One of my colleagues called, and I pulled over to talk to him. I was almost done and was about to leave." To support that claim, he started the engine.

Lyle didn't step back. Instead, he asked, "Have you talked to Aubrey? I was wondering how she was doing. I didn't want to bother her, though, if she has a lot going on."

The man was toying with Jonah, which made him furious. "The last time I spoke to her, she was fine."

That was no less than the truth. He kept his fingers crossed that she still was. "Well, I'd better get moving. Those crimes don't solve themselves, you know?"

The other man smirked, making Jonah want to deck him. "No, they don't. I know the police do their best, but sometimes that's just not enough. It's a real shame."

He was still smiling as he walked back toward the school. Jonah drove around the block and called the patrol officer who was due back from lunch soon. "Set up in a different location. Our target just paid me a visit, so he knows we're snooping around."

Then he hung up and headed back to the office, forgoing the stop to pick up sandwiches. They'd have to order in, because he had a feeling that he'd just thrown a wrench into Lyle's plans. Jonah was pretty sure Lyle wouldn't leave work early, because he'd been so careful to keep to his normal schedule. If he took off now, he had to be concerned that they'd simply follow him back to wherever he had Aubrey stashed. He was more likely to wait until darkness fell.

Either way, time was running out.

Aubrey slept fitfully for several hours and finally gave up on the effort to get any more sleep. Dark dreams didn't make for restful sleep. Instead, she once again practiced her yoga and martial arts routine. It was surprising how much the simple repetition cleared her head and gave her some sense of control. From what Lyle had said, he would make more than one additional visit to restock her supplies before the end of the school year. It wasn't that she didn't believe him about that. No, it was his intent to wait until his schedule was clear before the two of them would have fun together that she didn't believe.

That meant she needed to be ready for him. In between her naps, it crossed her mind that she could put the remaining cans of pop to good use. If she threw one right at him as soon as he stepped through the door, his first instinct would be to duck. If she could get the drop on him, she could club him with another can and then attack with her steel rod. If she could somehow render him unconscious, maybe she could get the key to her shackle. Once free, she could steal his car and head for civilization.

None of it would probably play out the way she envisioned, but she had to do something because time was growing short. Lyle would be coming soon. She left a can of pop sitting on top of the cooler and tucked the remaining two next to her on the bed where they couldn't be seen from the window. Satisfied she was as prepared as she would ever be, she settled back on the bed and watched as the sun started its slow descent to the west.

An hour passed and then another one. At least that was Aubrey's best guess. Time had ceased to have any real meaning to her by that point. She was considering eating another sandwich when she heard a vehicle approaching. It was tempting to run to the window to look out, but there was nothing to be gained by that. There was only one person who would be heading her way.

Sure enough, a short time later she heard footsteps outside of the door. She checked her makeshift weapons and braced herself for the fight to come.

The door slammed open, and Lyle stepped into the doorway. This time there was no slick charm in his demeanor, no attempt to be the affable principal she'd worked for. Instead, his face was all hard lines, and his pale gray eyes were glacial. "Your pet cop has been poking around and asking questions about me, Aubrey. I've spotted some of his buddies parked outside of the school, and my home security cameras have picked them up cruising by my condo hourly."

He took a single step forward into the cabin. "What did you tell him that set him on my trail?"

Aubrey refused to cower in the face of her captor's anger. "I didn't tell him anything about you other than you're the principal where I work. I didn't know you were involved until you showed up with the new supplies. If Detective Kelly suspects you, it's not because of anything I said or did."

"There had to be something, Aubrey. I can't risk another cop stumbling across the same information the next time."

She shuddered at the thought of some other innocent woman joining the ranks of Lyle's victims. All the more reason to do everything she could to put an end to his reign of terror. He was still waiting for her to confess how she'd managed to betray his secrets. If it could've bought her either time or mercy, she would've made something up. But the hatred glittering in his eyes made it clear that the clock was running out on her no matter what she told him.

"Like I said, I told him you were my boss. That's all."

He crossed his arms over his chest and planted his feet, probably hoping to further intimidate her. "So why did you take a leave of absence if not to get away from me?"

"Because we were worried that whoever was after me might try something at the school, which would put the kids and my coworkers in danger. It's the same reason I didn't go to stay with my parents or friends."

"Nothing about my private life?"

She shook her head. "No. Other than a few social gatherings with the rest of the staff, I've never spent time with you outside of work."

He abruptly gave up all pretense of being in control. He lunged across the narrow space and shoved her onto the bed. Aubrey screamed and tried to kick him with both feet, determined to keep him at bay. It took him a couple of tries to capture her right foot, but he finally managed. When she kicked him as hard as she could with her left, he jerked her off the bed onto to the floor and snarled, "If you want to save yourself some pain, stop it. I'm removing your shackle."

She froze, not sure if his doing that was actually a good thing. Regardless, there was no way she'd get free of him as long as she was chained to the bed. After he fished his keys out of his pocket, it took him a couple of tries to free her ankle. He let the chain drop to the floor and then jerked her back up to her feet. Holding on to both of her arms, he stared down at her.

"I put a lot of time and energy into planning my summer vacation, but you and your cop buddy have ruined it for me. Now I'm going to have to start all over with someone else. Not only that, I have to destroy my cabin and everything in it."

He leaned in closer to her face, close enough that she could feel his hot breath on her skin. "And then you're going to learn the answer to a question that you've been asking for twelve years—exactly where Marta ended up. I dug your grave right next to hers just over the next rise."

His smile was evil personified. "Remember how I flipped that coin? You were heads, and she was tails. Well, I lied about how it landed. It came up heads. I loved knowing you would live with the knowledge that it was only a matter of luck that you survived and your best friend didn't."

"But why?"

"Because she was my real target, not you. At least not then. I asked her out when she worked in the school library. Even tried to kiss her to show her how good it would be between us. She shoved me hard enough that I fell down. Then she stuck her hand in my face to show off that pitiful excuse for an engagement ring and threatened to tell her boyfriend if I didn't leave her alone. Right after that, she quit the job thinking that would deter me. We all know how well that worked for her."

He clearly took pride in the pain and misery he'd inflicted on so many people. Aubrey stared up at him in horror, seeing nothing human in his smile. "But enough about good times in the past. I have to deal with you and then get back to town before they realize I'm gone again."

He frowned. "Although it might be too late for that. Traffic was worse than I expected, and I've already been gone longer than I meant to be."

When he released his hold on her, she stumbled backward to sit down on the bed, this time on purpose. She wrapped her fingers around one of the pop cans she'd tucked under a fold in the blanket. Then she grasped her steel rod with her other hand.

"Stay there. I need a couple of things I left just outside the door."

When he turned his back to her, she almost went on the attack, but held back. Even if her efforts worked, he would be between her and the door. She watched as Lyle took a single step outside, and she knew she'd made the right decision. He came back in with two one-gallon cans of gasoline. He set one on top of the cooler, and then unscrewed the cap on the second and began splashing the gas on the walls. "Move away from the bed unless you would rather die in a fire."

Eyeing the second container of gas, she realized it would do more damage than the pop can. Still holding the rod next to her leg and out of sight, she sidestepped around the perimeter of the room, nearly choking on the gas fumes in the confined space. While he continued what he was doing, she drew a deep breath then grabbed the second gas can and swung as hard as she could at the back of his head.

Lyle bellowed in rage even as he dropped to his knees. That didn't keep him from scrambling after her on all fours, trying to block her escape. Before she could hit him a second time, he latched on to her ankle with one hand. At the same time, he wrapped his other arm around his head to prevent her second blow from connecting with full force.

When that didn't work, she stabbed his hand with the steel rod to force him to release his hold on her. When his hand fell open, she tried without success to pull the rod back out. It probably wasn't a good idea to leave her last weapon behind, but right now she was more concerned about putting some distance between herself and Lyle. He'd never completely lost consciousness, so she had seconds at best to get away. There was no chance she'd be able to steal the keys to his car without him getting his hands on her again. Praying she was making the best decision she could, she charged out into the night and ran like her life depended on it.

Because it did.

EIGHTEEN

Jonah paced the floor of the precinct, ready to explode. "What do you mean he's gone?"

The officer who was supposed to be watching the school had just called in to say that Lyle Peale was nowhere to be found.

"His SUV is still right where it's been all day, and the light is on in his office. A tow truck showed up about fifteen minutes ago and started loading up the car. It was the janitor who came out to give the guy the keys. I caught up with him to see where his boss was, only to learn Peale had already left. Supposedly, he'd told the janitor that his SUV wouldn't start when he tried to leave for lunch earlier in the day, and he'd made arrangements to have it taken to the dealership for repairs. He left his car keys with Jacobs to give the driver when he came."

"How long ago did Peale leave?"

"Jacobs thought the man planned to call a ride service to come pick him up, but he didn't actually see him go. Sounds like he was busy cleaning classrooms at the other end of the building from where the office is located. His best guess was that he'd last seen Peale about half an hour before the tow truck showed up. I can tell you for sure the principal didn't come out the front door. If he had, I would have seen him as well as the car that picked him up."

After a brief pause, the officer added, "I'm sorry, sir. He must have slipped out the back of the building and cut through to the road along the far end of the playground."

As angry as Jonah was, he knew the officer wasn't at fault. Peale was both smart and careful; otherwise someone would've caught him long before now. "You couldn't have known. Thanks for telling me."

He went back into the conference room to break the bad news. "Our target has flown the coop. He disappeared less than an hour ago, so he doesn't have much of a lead on us."

But they all knew how much damage a man could do to his victim in that amount of time. "We have to find him. We need a breakthrough right now."

Simply wishing for a solid clue that would lead them in the right direction wouldn't get them far. But maybe God had been listening, because Decker came running in with a map in his hand. He all but shoved it in Jonah's face. "We've found a small piece of property registered under his grandfather's name, Marcus Dennison. It's at the end of a forest service road in the foothills."

George spoke up next. "I just ran the sedan's plate number again. Seems our Mr. Peale must have been in a hurry after he left work. He got clocked going fifty in a thirty by a traffic camera. Judging from where that happened, he was headed toward the foothills, most likely via the interstate."

He walked around to study the map on the wall. "Here's where the camera picked him up."

Sergeant held his map up for comparison. "That jives with the most direct route to his property."

Maybe things were finally going their way. Jonah ordered, "Issue an alert on that vehicle with a warning to assume the driver is armed and dangerous. I'm going to update the captain and then head out."

George was already reaching for his jacket. "I'm coming, too."

Jonah didn't try to stop him. He headed for his boss's office and told him everything they'd learned. Captain Martine said he'd take care of getting help from the county and the state police. "Bring her back, Detective."

"I will, sir."

Five minutes later, he tore out of the parking lot, praying that Aubrey would hold on until he got there.

Aubrey ran past Lyle's car and kept going down the narrow road until it took a sharp bend to the left. With his longer legs, he would soon catch up with her if she continued much farther in plain sight. Picking a side at random, she plunged into the woods on the left side of the road and fought her way through the undergrowth. The sun rode low in the sky, barely providing her with enough light to see where she was going.

The smart thing would be to move as silently as possible, but she'd make better time running as fast and as far as she could. Getting lost was a huge risk, so she did her best to move parallel to the road. The only hope of survival she had was to find her way back toward civilization, or at least another road that would have more traffic on it.

"Aubrey! I will find you!"

Lyle's voice was faint, but there was no telling how sound traveled through the trees. She also had no sense of how far she'd come since she'd escaped from the cabin. Regardless, it was time to slow down and move with greater care. She needed to catch her breath as well as retain enough energy to put up a decent fight if he did catch up with her at some point.

A branch snapped back in her face, stinging and startling her into gasping. She blinked past the tears and kept moving, even as she heard Lyle calling her name from off to her right. He was still behind her, but closer now. It was time to start looking for a weapon to replace the one she'd left behind. A big stick wouldn't be much protection from a gun if he had one, but she needed something.

"Aubrey, I'm coming for you!"

By that point, Lyle's voice was less angry and more gleeful, as if this was a game that had become fun for him. She picked up a hefty branch and took cover in the center of a cluster of bushes, waiting for the battle to begin. The only question was which role she would play in their game— the cat or the mouse.

Jonah reached the turnoff to the forest service road in better time than he'd expected. Other cars on the highway had cooperated and got out of his way in response to his flashing lights and the occasional blast from his siren. A county deputy had joined their parade a short time before they'd turned off the highway. Once they'd left the highway behind, Jonah drove as fast as he deemed safe, which apparently was at a higher speed than his companion was comfortable with, considering the death grip George had on the bar over the passenger door.

"'Hanging in there okay, Detective?"

The other man laughed a little. "I'll survive. Maybe, anyway."

"We should reach the turnoff to Peale's property soon. I'm guessing I'll have to slow down on it."

He was pretty sure George muttered, "I hope so."

As it turned out, Jonah had no choice but to actually stop after they turned onto the driveway that should lead them to the cabin. A short distance down the dirt road, there was a gate that spanned the entire width. It was made of heavy-duty steel pipe and fastened with a massive padlock.

Jonah stared at it as George asked, "Do you have a bolt cutter?"

"No, I'll ask the deputy."

Deputy Hicklin had one, but it wouldn't handle a lock with a shackle that thick. "I'll call for the fire department to send someone out with one of theirs."

"How long will that take?"

Hicklin didn't look optimistic. "Half an hour minimum."

"I can't wait that long. You two wait here while I go ahead on foot. Peale had a big head start, so he's already here. Ms. Sims might not have thirty minutes."

George wasn't happy about his decision. "More backup is already on the way. You shouldn't go in alone."

He was right. Jonah didn't care. "Tell them to be careful who they're targeting when they start after us. I have my phone on mute but I'll check for texts as I can, if we even get service up here."

Then he climbed the gate and took off running along the dirt road toward the cabin. His knee protested, but he ignored it and kept pounding down the road at a steady pace. Suddenly, he heard Peale calling out that he was coming for Aubrey. Jonah followed the sound off to his right, holding his gun down at his side as he changed course and started working his way through the trees.

He'd gone about a hundred feet when he heard Aubrey scream. It came from close by, and he thought he caught a glimpse of movement through the trees too far away to get a clear shot. Jonah slowed down enough to make sure he didn't alert Peale to his presence as he closed in on the enemy.

When Jonah reached a small clearing, Aubrey and Peale were circling each other. When Peale lunged for her, she swung for the bleachers with a thick branch, aiming for the man's head, but connecting with his shoulder instead. She managed to put maybe twenty feet between them, but the man was already up and lumbering after her.

"You'll die for that, Aubrey." He waved his gun in the air. "I'll bury you alive, which will give you plenty of time to reflect on your mistakes."

She continued to back away from him, still clutching her makeshift weapon. When Peale took aim at her, Jonah didn't hesitate. The shot left Lyle Peale writhing on the ground and holding his leg.

"Stay back, Aubrey," Jonah ordered as he approached the wounded man. He tossed Peale's gun out of reach. Then he holstered his own weapon and rolled Peale over on his stomach before kneeling down to handcuff him, ending the threat to Aubrey once and for all. Having secured his prisoner, Jonah removed his jacket and then his shirt. He wrapped the latter around the man's wounded leg and yanked it tight.

Pushing himself back up to his feet, he turned toward Aubrey and held out his arms. She came running straight toward him, reaching him just as his knee almost gave out on him.

He held her close. "Are you okay, Aubrey? Did he hurt you?"

"Bruises, nothing else." She stared up at him with tears glistening in her eyes. "You came for me. I prayed you would."

Then she kissed him.

He wanted to hold her forever, to kiss her until all these ugly memories faded into the past, but he had other obligations right now. He led her to a fallen log and wrapped his jacket around her shoulders. "Stay here while I call for backup and the EMTs to come deal with Peale."

She did as he asked. "George, Aubrey and I are both fine. Notify the EMTs that the target is down with a gunshot to his lower leg. Bring a blanket and the first aid kit from my car. We're off the right side of the road about a quarter mile up from where I left you. When you get close, start shouting, and I'll answer."

He went back over to keep an eye on his prisoner. As he did, he had something to say to Aubrey before the cavalry arrived. "After we get this situation handled, we need to talk about us and the future. It's going to involve words like love, marriage and forever. You okay with that?"

At first, her answering smile was a bit tremulous, but it grew in strength. "I can't wait."

EPILOGUE

The next twenty-four hours were a blur for Aubrey, mainly because she'd ended up in the hospital for observation. Her parents had arrived shortly after she'd been moved to a private room where they'd had an emotional reunion. An hour later, the nurses finally told her folks that visiting hours were over for the night.

Before they left, all three of them had shared prayers of thanksgiving that the ordeal was now over and that Aubrey was finally safe. To her surprise, Jonah's name had played a significant role in her mother's message to God, thanking Him for bringing Detective Kelly into their lives right when they'd needed him the most.

That was good, because if it was up to Aubrey, he'd be sticking around a lot longer—preferably permanently. Not that she'd seen him since the ambulance had whisked her away from the crime scene. That didn't surprise her. He had a job to do, an important one. He'd told her he had to stick around to deal with the crime scene, starting with the cabin. At least Lyle hadn't had a chance to set it on fire once she took off running.

Once the initial hubbub slowed down a bit, she remembered to tell him what Lyle had said about having dug a grave for Aubrey right next to Marta's. From what she understood, the authorities would wait until morning to start the search. Since Lyle had mentioned to Aubrey that he'd entertained other guests, they would also look for other unmarked graves.

It was sad and sick, but it was over. At least the Pynes and Ross Easton would finally have the closure they so badly needed. That was something else she'd thanked God for.

She'd already signed her discharge papers and was waiting for her parents to come pick her up. But when the door opened, it was Jonah standing there. He looked exhausted, but that didn't stop him from sweeping her up in his arms and holding her so tightly she could barely breathe. That was okay—they both needed the reassurance that they'd made it through the ordeal alive and whole.

When he finally set her back down, she had to ask one question. "Did you find her?"

He nodded. "Right where you said she'd be. We've already reached out to her parents and Ross even though it won't be official until we get the DNA tests back."

"I'm happy for them. They've waited a long time for closure."

"George Swahn asked to be the one who delivered the news. He was thrilled to close one of his files."

"I can understand why. He's worked so hard to bring answers to the people who need them the most."

Jonah hesitated as if he was reluctant to tell her something. Finally, he said, "About that—working the cold cases was supposed to be a temporary job for me. You know, just until my knee improves. I've already told Captain Martine I want the assignment long-term. I hope that's okay with you."

Now she was confused. "Why would what I think matter?"

His blue eyes twinkled with a hint of mischief. "Because I figure my future wife should have a say in my plans. Not that I'm exactly proposing. I figure we should go on a few dates first."

He looked stricken when she couldn't stop the tears from coming. He brushed them away with the pad of his thumb. "Honey, I didn't mean to rush you. We can take things as slow as you need to."

Silly man. "I'm not upset, Jonah. I'm really happy! This is the first time I've had a chance to plan for the future instead of being mired in my past. I can't wait to see where you take me on our first date."

"Maybe church on Sunday? And then out to a late breakfast with your folks? Of course, my parents will want equal time the next weekend."

"That sounds perfect!"

Then she kissed him to seal the deal.

* * * * *